*To the students who sat in my classroom:*

*I hope you found your voice and realized that you—not the data—are what matters. May your pulse always beat for the truth, and may you never choose the safety of silence.*

**Published January 19, 2026**
**Published by Pine Veil Press**

ISBN (print): 978-1-971147-00-0
ISBN (ebook): 978-1-971147-01-7

Cover design by Dana Perich

Printed in the United States of America

# Table of Contents

# Chapter 1

Every adult insists we've got it better than anyone before us. They act like we should bleed gratitude just because we don't wake to bombs or famine. Maybe they're right. But when Mr. Everett starts his lecture, I don't hear gratitude. I hear a warning.

"The world is always ending, but it never truly ends; the circumstances merely shift. Every generation believes they are the last—convinced that their specific war, their specific famine, is the final act. They are always wrong."

Mr. Everett launches into the usual diatribe, hitting all the predictable beats: the chaos of the 2028 election, the panic during COVID-19 pandemic, the hunger of the Great Depression. He treats history like a list of reasons to stay quiet. He stops mid-sentence, not because he's finished but because his lungs demand it. He doesn't pause—he fights for air, dragging in a deep, shuddering breath.

I don't just know this tirade; it's written into my genetic code. The words didn't start in this classroom—they coiled around my DNA in my grandmother's living room long before they became a routine lecture in the syllabus. While the core message is always the same, the details shift each time. Some versions highlight the noteworthy struggles of generations before us. Others linger on the sustainable progress achieved since the Twenty-Ninth Amendment was ratified in 2036.

Inevitably, they bring up how under the current rules we've reached perfect stability; we no longer have to worry. I let the specifics blur. Instead, I feel the subtext—that cold, blurring layer of condensation smeared across every word. It makes the classroom feel damp, like the walls are closing in.

The fundamental message: be grateful for what you've reaped due to others' suffering.

I'm sure most of the other kids are sick of it by now. After seventeen or eighteen years of hearing the same message almost verbatim, it can get old, but I revel in the predictability. By senior year, I know the script by heart. I let the familiarity settle. It doesn't matter if it's a formal lesson or a teacher's provoked outburst—the words never change.

Usually those words are a response to someone like Silas. He's the one who baits Mr. Everett, nursing some dark fantasy about anarchy and uprisings. Every time he leans forward to goad Mr. Everett, my skin prickles. It's absurd; the world hasn't seen a shred of unrest since my great-grandparents were in school, yet Silas acts like he's ready to set fire to the floorboards. I find myself wishing he'd just stay silent and let the stability hold.

Before Mr. Everett loses his momentum or the attention of the class, he launches back into his speech. As if on cue, he fires off, "Your generation is no different," chopping the air with his hand. "You have it better than you could ever imagine. But no Silas," he stares right at him, "the world is not coming to an end despite your grand delusions at seventeen."

There it is.

The final, predictable point. We are ignorant. We are naive. And for those very reasons, we should be grateful.

Mr. Everett's rant is a direct insult to my entire generation.

Austin rolls his eyes and Cody fades into the wall, but I anchor myself to my seat. I remain the sole outlier, refusing to flinch. I offer no resistance because I have no desire to fight. Because the truth is, Mr. Everett is right. Our reality is idyllic—and the thought of a single crack forming in that perfection makes my lungs tighten.

The script didn't start with Mr. Everett; it started with the people who built this world. The image of my grandparents, sitting rigid and satisfied in their living room, flashes sharply into focus. It pulls me away from the classroom noise, dissolving the droning voice of Mr. Everett until it becomes the comfortable hum of an old television.

# Chapter 2

My favorite childhood memories are watching historical documentaries with my grandmother and my brother, James. Every Friday, our whole family would walk the four blocks to their house for dinner, and then my parents would leave my brother and me with Gran and Gramps.

We bypassed the board games for the television, submerging ourselves in historical records. Gramps' rhythmic snoring became the white noise of our education. James and I sat motionless, captivated not by the production, but by the anticipation of the aftermath. Gran's commentary turned the documentaries into skeletons; she provided the flesh. Her stories spanned a century of collapse and restructuring—the 2020 pandemic through the 2036 Amendment. That wasn't just history; it was a blueprint.

If we were lucky, Gran would walk to the overstuffed bookshelf, the floorboards groaning beneath her, and pull out one of her heavy plastic-sleeved scrapbooks. She'd set the book down on the coffee table and recite one of her mantras: "To preserve order, we must keep an accurate account of history."

As we grew older, James and I would lean forward and say the words along with her. It always felt like a simple "Gran-ism," a saying unique to her, but the older I've gotten, the more these same sentiments have been reiterated, especially here in school.

Gran would show us photos she had meticulously cataloged—her own snapshots, along with yellowed, hastily taped pictures kept by her parents and grandparents. Her family has lived in the Lynn area for generations, and the sheer visual difference between those photos and the Lynn I know today is jarring.

After nearly thirteen years of schooling, it's still a shock each time I exit a school building. The pristine interior of Classical High stops at the door. Outside, Lynn remains a graveyard. The city stopped pouring concrete for the public years ago, choosing instead to rebuild only what mattered: the schools, the nuclear family, and the government hubs. Everything else is just a skeletal remain, shadows of the city my great-grandparents knew.

As kids, we would beg for more, our hands reaching for the pages. But she always steered us back, ensuring every photograph was tied to the message of the night's documentary. If we were too greedy, she'd simply offer our second favorite Gran-ism: "Too much of anything isn't good for anyone."

Gran full-heartedly believes this, not just for children, but for everyone. Too much information, or too much freedom, leads to brash decisions and abused liberty. Her stories and Friday night films were built on a single foundation: preserving history to avoid repeating it.

It's why they named us what they did: names chosen for American icons, like my dad, Lincoln, or great-American places—Denver or Virginia. My brother, James, was named after Jamestown and I was named Alexandria for the Virginian City. It shows a sense of patriotism, a reverence for the past folded into the new American dream set forth by the Twenty-Ninth Amendment.

Our history—that legacy—is why Gran's stories captivate me most. They happened to people in our family, to people related to me. In a life where I'm usually a ghost, Gran makes me feel seen. Hearing her stories is the one time I have a sense of purpose—a feeling I might actually matter.

It's why, when everyone else is rolling their eyes or zoning out, I catch my head in a slow, involuntary nod of agreement with each one of Mr. Everett's points. I stifle the movement. I doubt anyone's paying attention to me, but I don't need to add 'brownnoser' to the list of reasons my classmates don't like me.

It doesn't matter that I'm eighteen; I'm still counting down the hours until tomorrow night. After cross-country practice, I'll travel the four blocks to Gran and Gramps' house, like I have since I was small.

The family dinners ended years ago. James's teenage years became a slow-motion vanishing act. School and work gave him the perfect excuse to trade our Friday rituals for a world where he didn't have to watch our parents pretend. I kept going though, always alone. I used the distance for sprint practice—a form of desperate therapy.

I pounded the pavement, trying to outrun the echoes of the fights Mom and Dad thought I couldn't hear. My sneakers slapped against the uneven asphalt, and I had to time my strides to leap over the deep fissures snaking across the sidewalk. It was a strange, jagged commute—sprinting through the ruins of the old world just to reach the polished safety of the new one.

The security within Gran's walls is real, but even our time there is a fragmented version of what it once was. We still eat dinner, still watch a documentary, and Gramps still dozes off, his snoring a reliable comfort. Gran tells her stories and pulls out scrapbooks, though every page is a repeat after so many years.

My parents were performance artists, maintaining the hollowed-out shell of a marriage that looked as pristine as the glass in my school. But inside, the rot was absolute. Mom's normalcy was a mechanical routine—sealing leftovers, setting the table, and pretending the silence wasn't a scream.

The fighting was confined to their bedroom, but their words were ferocious. James and I would press ourselves against the opposite wall, unable to make out every word. We would catch pieces, though. Mom accused him of lying about his late nights. Dad would counter dismissively, calling her paranoid and useless.

I froze outside their door. It was cracked barely enough for the words to slice through.

"You better keep your pants," Mom's voice was a jagged blade, "because your vasectomy was reversed long ago. You didn't just lie to me, Lincoln. How many other children are you planning to saddle with your 'emotional uninvestment'?"

When they emerged, the faces they wore were smooth and blank. Mom would ask me to help her set the table. If James was home, Dad would put him to work taking out the trash, then retreat behind a documentary or a book until the meal was ready. Sometimes Dad wouldn't even come home until hours after we'd finished. Mom would act unfazed, robotically sealing his portion of food into a container and sliding it into the refrigerator.

After dinner, I'd bolt upstairs, shove my earbuds in, cranking the volume until the world outside my skull went mute. At ten, Gran's favorites were the only songs I knew. Gran inherits a love of pop from her own mother, and to this day, Taylor Swift's 'Shake It Off' and Miley Cyrus's 'Party in the U.S.A.' are personal favorites. Most kids my age would make fun of me for listening to them. James used to tease me mercilessly.

But these songs remind me of a happier time. They're my escape—a chance to dance through the chaos. I'll take simple, positive oldies over the melodrama James and my classmates listen to any day.

My life is already a wreck; I don't need my music to prove it.

Everything during that period is a blur—a hazy collection of arguments and passive-aggressive silences. I'd stay alone in my room, playing dead until the faint sound of Dad's tires hit the driveway.

One specific night stands out: days before James's graduation, both my favorite and my worst.

James had recently turned eighteen and was set to graduate high school the next week. The night before he casually dropped the bomb: he planned to move to Boston over the weekend for a full-time job at the Sterilization Facility, his current part-time gig.

The words themselves felt cold, efficient, and important—like something that belonged entirely to Boston and the grown-up world I wasn't ready for. I didn't know exactly what he did there, but I knew it was important.

I thought I had more time. Even though school ended on Friday, the ceremony was Tuesday. He shrugged, saying he didn't need the ceremony; he had the diploma and the job.

I was only eleven. The thought of him leaving me alone with Mom and Dad felt like abandonment. Lynn is thirty-five minutes from Boston, but at that age, it felt like light years.

The last dinner at Gran and Gramps' house became my singular obsession for the next twenty-four hours. It crowded out every other thought. When I raced home from school the next afternoon, I found James already mid-departure, packing boxes into his car with a frantic energy.

The moment I stepped through the door, the air felt wrong. Something was off.

It was unusual to find Dad home at this hour, but he stood in the kitchen with disheveled hair, one side sticking up from his restless hands. The silence between him and Mom wasn't the usual hostile calm —it was the ringing aftermath of a bomb.

Struck between my desperate hope for one last dinner and the palpable tension, I asked earnestly, "Did you come home early so we could go over to Gran and Gramps' now?"

Dad stared at me for an agonizing moment, his face a blank mask.

Mom was flushed crimson. She threw her hands up in an exaggerated gesture. "Why don't you tell her, Lincoln Eastwick? You didn't come home early to spend time as a family, but to destroy our family, you lying piece of shit."

Her words shocked me. Aside from the one muffled fight I'd overheard through the cracked door, Mom didn't talk like that.

"Wh-wh-what are you talking about?" My voice was a fragile mumble. "Aren't we going to go to Gran and Gramps' for dinner?"

Mom's face was inches from Dad's, her eyes filled with a fury I didn't know she possessed. "Not only did your Dad fuck another woman when he was 'working late,' but get this," she spat, her voice loaded with acid, "you're going to be a big sister—not to one baby but to two."

I know it's his fault. He's the one I should be mad at, but I still struggle with resentment for the way my mom delivered the news. Being an older sister is supposed to be exciting. Instead, it was tainted from the very beginning.

I wondered if James saw the irony. While he was moving to a city to help manage the population, our father was back in Lynn, busily overpopulating it. It felt like a sick joke: James was going to work for a system designed to keep life clean and controlled, while our own house was becoming a breeding ground for the very mess the Twenty-Ninth Amendment was meant to fix.

She stared at Dad, the words dripping with venom. "The system truly is fucked up if it said you were competent enough to have children. Maybe you should have taken James's new job—at least then you'd be doing the world a favor by stopping yourself."

This was Mom's first and final act of rebellion. She never had before, and she never would again.

So much for Gran's order. This wasn't history; it was chaos. I didn't stay to hear anymore. I bolted.

I ran for James, desperate to see if he was still the brother I knew or if he had already become a part of that cold, efficient world. I needed him to be a shield, to tell me the 'bomb' wasn't real. But he was already half-way in his car, his face as blank as the pristine interior of my school. "I can't do this anymore," he said, slamming the door shut. He didn't look at me. He didn't offer a seat. He was already a ghost.

Abandoned, my last resort was four blocks away.

I sprinted the entire distance, my lungs burning, not knowing what I would say. The "Party in the U.S.A." beat I usually ran to was gone, replaced by the ringing in my ears from my mother's voice. When I got there, I didn't even knock. I turned the knob and pushed the door open.

Gran was already at the table, two places set. The house didn't smell like smoldering wreckage; it smelled like roast chicken and floor wax. She didn't look surprised and she didn't ask questions. She simply looked up and said, "I was hoping you'd still come for dinner."

She didn't need to hear the words. The way I was shaking told the story for me. That was enough—proof Gran knew. No explanations needed. No talking. I could escape the chaos here, surrounded by everything comfortable and predictable.

Gran took pity on me all evening, clearly abandoning her mantra, "Too much of anything isn't good for anyone." For that one night, the rules were suspended. She let me fill the hollowed-out shell of my chest with sugar and starch. I skipped the vegetables, went back for seconds, and had three helpings of dessert. Gran didn't encourage the gluttony, but she didn't stop me and she didn't shame me. She must have been processing, too.

She indulged me, not with food, but with history.

Normally after one story or a handful of photos, I was cut off. But tonight, Gran opened more albums. Gramps even chimed in. I saw photos of massive yard signs and flags from the twenty-first century: 'Save America,' and 'Make America Great Again.' Some showed politicians' faces photoshopped onto absurdly buff bodies or cars.

Gran told me about her grandfather, Ryan, and the slogans he kept everywhere—on his car, his hats, his house. He lived his life out loud, just like the people on the flags, with no filter and no restraint. But she also acknowledged the truth: her grandfather was a part of the problem. He fathered four children by three women but funded the lives of just two of his kids: my great-grandmother Lizzy and her brother David. He chased every new gadget, running up his credit cards to make his car faster or his TV louder.

Gran had never shared this much about her family before. I leaned in, hungry for any detail of how life had changed after President Wolf's election in 2028, when Gramps finally gave his two cents.

"Americans were always looking for someone to fix the problems," Gramps interjected, leaning forward in his chair. His voice was steady, a sharp contrast to the shouting still echoing in my mind. "Poverty, gun violence, broken homes, debt, homelessness—whatever it was. But they always had the wrong solution: people rather than laws. It wasn't President Wolf who changed America; the Twenty-Ninth Amendment transformed this country into what it is today."

Gran nodded, closing the photo album with a soft thud. "A good place to stop. Remember, Alexandria, the Twenty-Ninth Amendment is the difference between my parents' world and yours."

She stood up, pulling on her coat. "I'll walk you home."

Gran has always been the unquestioned matriarch. What she says goes. When she says it's time to go, it is. Despite my yearning to hear more, I knew the night was over. The "too much" had been reached.

I will never forget that night—the moment the chasm in my family grew beyond repair. I learned my ancestors were a contributing part of the problem, and my dad was repeating the cycle. Watching Gran zip her coat, I realized I couldn't be like them. I refused to be the problem. I needed to be the solution, dedicated to upholding this better place for future generations.

# Chapter 3

I have one real complaint about Mr. Everett's lecture. He might be forty, if that, but he acts as though the need for gratitude applies only to those of us sitting in these seats. He doesn't know any better, either. He didn't live through overpopulation, broken families, war, gun violence, or homelessness. He's lecturing as if he survived a time of national instability, but he's a child of the Amendment—born into the safety we're forced to thank him for. He needs to realize how good he has it too.

"Next time you think about derailing class, Silas, come up with something a bit more realistic so it can at least be a debate and not a waste of everyone's time. Now let's get back to the project, shall we?"

Silas doesn't flinch at the backlash. I thought I even caught a subtle smirk beneath the swoop of his black bangs—hair that acts as a mask, shrouding the left side of his face. Silas has always kept an even-keeled and unreadable composure.

Living on the outskirts of Boston, where the population has steadily declined, it's impossible not to know everyone. Silas and I have shared a classroom since kindergarten, though for years he was simply a background actor in my life. Now, he commands the stage, and I'm the one fading into the scenery.

Our first real interaction didn't happen until fifth grade. Back then, he wore his dark hair in a buzz cut—a practical choice for the parents of an athlete.

And that's where it happened—on the playground baseball field.

---

It was the end-of-year teacher versus student kickball game, a tradition structured to involve the right amount of cardio for the middle-aged staff. Silas and I were both athletic, playing sports all year round. We wouldn't have chosen kickball, but neither of us tolerated losing. We both knew beating the teachers required us to carry the slackers. This was years before the DPU—the District Performance Unit —became a mandatory weight on our waistbands, but even then, the pressure to prove our physical 'viability' haunted every competition. Even at ten, we knew the state was always watching, measuring our worth.

I'd seen him picked first in enough gym class to recognize an ally. Winning required strategizing the whole gamut: lineups, positions, and peer placement. So before the game started, I walked up and presented my plan.

Was he interested, or just dealing with me? Was he dissecting every word? His face gave nothing away, but by the end, we had an alliance: I would cover most of the infield from shortstop, and he would handle most of the outfield from center field. We put our most adequate classmates in the backup spots. It wasn't foolproof, but it was the best we could muster.

The game progressed perfectly. We were up 3-1with one inning left. Silas made a couple of great outfield catches, and I turned a clutch double play. Even timid Cody, feeding off the momentum, snagged an important third-out infield catch with the bases loaded.

We went into the final inning feeling confident. Silas had maintained a perfect balance of assuredness and calm throughout the game; only when I executed the double-play did I detect a slight, fleeting spark of excitement in his eyes.

With two outs and Mr. K and Ms. Nelson on base, Mrs. Baker was up for the fourth time. She hesitated on all her previous kicks, sending the ball close to the third baseline. I inched up and over, bent at the knees, my entire body anticipating the ball's trajectory.

As expected, the ball came slightly inside the third baseline. I sprinted in low, ready to scoop it up —but then the ball struck a rock or dirt patch. Whatever it was, it bounced and flew completely off course. I fell into the dirt, reaching for empty air.

It zipped past me and into the outfield. Mr. K scored. Ms. Nelson was rounding third when Silas grabbed the ball. Mrs. Baker was in a pickle between second and third, and Ms. Nelson between third and home. The pressure was entirely on Silas. If the throw failed, the game would be tied and we'd have to go into extra innings. The worst case? An error that would let Mrs. Baker score and hand the teachers the win.

I was humiliated, lying face down in the dirt, proving my inability to deliver clutch, calculated action. From the ground, I watched Silas fake out Mrs. Baker. Instead of throwing the ball to one of our classmates, he controlled the entire exchange. As Ms. Nelson was inches from scoring, everything seemed to shift into slow motion.

This was the biggest moment of my elementary career, and I was wallowing in the dirt. Silas, however, was laser-focused, a predator taking on his prey, his eyes locked on Mrs. Baker. It was a glimpse of the person he was becoming—the version of Silas that doesn't just play the game, but manipulates it.

With one swift, decisive swing of his arm, he released the ball.

It struck her square in the stomach when she was centimeters shy of second base. Out.

The entire class erupted, swarming Silas. We won 3-2, not because of me, but because of him.

Any normal ten-year-old boy would have bragged and embellished. But Silas remained unruffled. There was obvious pride, but he never bragged or put himself above any of the other kids. When I finally stood up caked in dirt, he was above me, meeting my gaze and offering a silent, firm handshake—thanking me for my minimal contribution. No verbal exchange, just the swap of a hand.

He walked away, knowing he'd covered my fatal mistake. It shouldn't have been so close. My pride had clouded my vision and compromised my ability, forcing him to intervene and save the day.

The kickball game marked our first and last one-on-one exchange.

Silas has changed outwardly. He is still athletic and competitive, but the long hair masks his features, keeping him distant. Yet, in many ways, he is the same: confident, unreadable, and daring. I saw the predator in him once on a dusty kickball field, and now, I see it every time he smirks at a lecture. He isn't afraid of the world breaking; he's waiting for it.

Since fifth grade, his mere presence makes me doubt myself, making me feel small and inconsequential. It affirms every ounce of insecurity and every thought of inadequacy. Silas's silence speaks volumes, and I'm not sure he even knows the weight of it.

"Presentations start tomorrow," Mr. Everett says, rushing to find his point. "If we forget the past, we lose our stability." He fights to reel us back in, but the bell wins. Its shrill scream drowns him out.

# Chapter 4

Outside of History, I am nothing more than an average student. My talent manifests solely during a run. I anchor my life to it: cross-country in the fall and track in the spring. Unfortunately, Massachusetts's winters force everything indoors. Freshman year, I had to choose between basketball and swimming for my winter sport. The fifth grade kickball fiasco taught me early on that I was better suited for individual competitions, so swimming was the lesser of two evils.

Fall is my favorite time of year. It's cross-country season, and long distances are my forte. Once I get moving, I enter a zone. My body finds a rhythm, and my mind soon blanks out, focused on the thumping beat of each foot hitting the concrete, one after another. The repetition is soothing; I crave the monotony of the run. It's one of the few times I can escape my own thoughts.

The air is crisp—biting, but refreshing. There is nothing like the cold air hitting my face and the sharp sting entering my lungs. It doesn't matter how much I sweat; I always smell like autumn—arguably the best scent on earth.

In an ideal world, I could run or swim and never worry about anyone else. But these are all team-based. We don't score points together, but we still work toward a common goal, a shared victory.

This is nearly impossible when you fundamentally don't get along with other people. I'm used to the isolation—the whispering behind my back or the complete, dismissive silence. I'm never sure which I prefer. The whispers remind me I'm visible. Still, it's hard to swallow being called a blight on the town—living proof the Twenty-Ninth Amendment is necessary.

Somehow, even with my minimal friendships, the absurd rumors find me: the one about my dad, at twenty-five, using his position at the Testing Center of Massachusetts to electronically change his benchmark status to 'passed.' I doubt it's possible—he's worked there forever—but people love to talk. The rumors are endless, yet rarely said to my face. It's always in the locker room, delivered by people who don't realize how loud their 'whispers' are, or those who assume I'm too far inside the shower stall to hear every word.

It's hard enough not to punch someone in the face when they're trash-talking you, let alone work on a team. This makes practice days my favorite. The goal is simple: everyone works for their personal best. There's no pretense of encouragement, no bus ride together, no quality time required. No winning or losing means no blame game. On practice days, I don't have to worry about the competition or my teammates. My only obligation is my own rhythm.

"In our last competition, the DPU recorded a 15% dip in efficiency. We need to fix the data." Coach Vance's gaze snaps from his clipboard directly to me.

The DPU—that sleek, black plastic clip—bites into the waistband of my shorts, a cold reminder that my earlier fears on the playground have finally taken physical form. This season, the Unit isn't just a threat; it's a mandate. It's the size of a thumb drive, but as I stand there, it carries the weight of a judge.

We were told it tracked 'oxygen efficiency and fatigue markers' to secure a major new funding grant. The sterile number was a verdict I couldn't argue with, a concrete measurement of my failure.

I can't tell if it's intentional, but Coach Vance hasn't discussed Tuesday's meet. I placed first, yes, but it wasn't a personal best. I struggled to maintain pace toward the finish and scarcely won by 2.8 seconds when I should have crushed the competition. The other coaches and team congratulated me, but no one on my own team even acknowledged the victory.

Coach Vance's eyes sweep across the rest of the huddle. "Others started too weak and fell behind early on."

I see Mariah self-consciously dart her eyes away. She is our second-best runner and usually my most challenging competition, though I beat her consistently. She struggled last week, finishing fifth overall when she easily should have been third. She needs this sport to work, like I do; a dip in efficiency likely threatens her compliance status.

My narrow win and Mariah's low placement cost us the team win, a disappointing and unexpected result. Whether it was the new course layout or a simple internal malfunction that caused the dip, Coach's silence on the bus ride home communicated a single warning: it couldn't be a repeat offense.

"The starting target is to find your speed somewhere between sixty and eighty percent. This will help you maintain endurance throughout and push the limit when you need to be at maximum speed." Coach Vance takes a necessary, deep breath, slowing for a moment. "But you know all of this. You've been doing it for years."

His voice suddenly picks up in volume and agitation. For as silent as he was on Tuesday, he's making up for it now. He's clearly processed his frustration and reached a verdict. I'm not sure where he's going. We all know the tempo techniques; Mariah and I, especially, have been drilling them for years in our final season.

"You know what the problem is? This team doesn't behave like a team. There's no communication, no camaraderie. Well, that's about to change."

Oh God. This is exactly why I joined cross-country—to avoid this. I have no interest in team-bonding, and even less interest in mandated camaraderie.

"If we're going to lose as a team, we better start acting like one. So today we will not be running. We will be partaking in team building activities."

I'm typically eager to appease adults and maintain a strained civility with my peers, but this is a step too far. Between Mr. Everett's rant and Coach Vance's outburst today, I'm starting to believe every adult in this school is suffering from a superiority complex. First, Mr. Everett wants me to be a grateful drone; now Coach Vance wants me to give up the one thing belonging solely to me. They all want to control the stability, but I need a place to escape it.

# Chapter 5

The announcement is met by a collective, audible groan—a sound I join, for once, with full conviction.

Coach Vance makes us stand in a circle, close our eyes, and shove our hands into the middle. When we open them, each of us is clutching two different hands, forming a tangled, chaotic human knot. "Now, without letting go," he instructs, "try to detangle yourselves."

Ashley and Alicia—the self-appointed, high-pitched top dogs of the junior class—immediately start barking competing orders. Everyone is interrupting and no one is listening to each other. I scan the blur of sweaty bodies and strained arms, but can't meet a single person's eye. My blood pressure spikes. I thrive on predictability and routine. Cross country practice is supposed to be my refuge; today, it's my own personal hell.

"Shut up!"

The roar of voices immediately drops to a stunned murmur. "Instead of everyone shouting," I clip out, feeling the heat rise in my cheeks, "can one person speak and give directions? Then maybe we can get this over with."

The silence that follows is thick and accusatory. I can feel the eyes of my teammates drilling into me. I've spent years priding myself on being the girl who nods in agreement with the rules of order, yet here I am, becoming the very friction I hate. The heat in my face isn't just embarrassment; it's the burning realization that I've let the 'uncontrollable' part of me win.

It takes a moment for the silence to break. Then, Mariah takes the lead, "Alicia, untangle your right arm first, then your left."

Alicia maneuvers herself out. She ends up facing outward, her arms stretched rigid, holding onto Mariah and a freshman named Casey. Mariah follows, then Coach Vance, until finally, the whole team is a giant circle holding hands, a patchwork of faces looking inward and outward.

"It took a while, but you did it. You defeated the Human Knot. Round one is complete. Two more rounds to go."

I nearly scream again. After such a pathetic display, he can't be serious. A few whines rise up, and I feel a brief inward sense of camaraderie, knowing my irritation isn't a solo act.

Coach pulls out a blue tarp and lays it flat on the grass. "Everyone come and stand on the tarp."

A few eager people jog over, but the rest of us move with a deliberate slowness—an irony for a group built on speed. Coach doesn't yell; he waits.

"Think of this tarp as a magic carpet. The goal is to flip the carpet to the other side without stepping off. If anyone touches the field, you start over. By the end, the carpet should be completely reversed, and you should all be standing on it."

"Where does he come up with this shit?" I hear Casey whisper to a freshman beside her. Her words mirror my thoughts. Maybe I am more like my teammates than I think.

This time the shouting is minimal. Mariah continues to direct, though it's obvious she's simply echoing Ashley's ideas. Ashley, having learned from the Human Knot, has wisely stayed quieter this round.

"Everyone, move toward the back corner," Mariah directs, her voice gentle but confident. As we shift, the proximity becomes more and more suffocating. Hair brushes my cheek, my ass is up against someone else, and I feel a warm breath on my neck. Suddenly, someone grabs my waist for stability, but the effort fails. Instead, we both tumble. The grass is cool, but the humiliation is hot. This is exactly what happens when you tether your stability to the clumsy feet of others.

"Start over," Coach Vance states flatly.

So we're back to square one. This time, Ashley helps Mariah more overtly. We have to restart once more before we manage to flip the carpet within minutes.

"Congratulations on completing your magic carpet ride. Much better than the Human Knot."

I detect a tinge of joy as Coach Vance announces the last activity. "For this one, you will be partnered up."

Everyone immediately shuffles toward their friends. I stand perfectly still.

"I will be partnering you up, so you can stop where you are," he corrects the team.

"One of you will be blindfolded, and the other will be placed randomly on the field. The goal is for the blindfolded person to find their teammate simply from the sound of their voice."

I swear Coach's sole goal today is to torture us so badly we never lose again.

"Ashley and Casey, Mariah and Alexandria," Coach starts rattling off names, but I only hear the first two. Of all people to be paired with, why did it have to be Mariah?

I can feel her eyes on me, likely searching for a flicker of the competitive heat she expects. She probably assumes I hate her because she's the closest thing to competition I have on this team. She may view me as a rival, but I don't see her as one. It's not pride; it is simply fact. She constantly strives to beat me, but I don't need to try to beat her. In four years she outperformed me once when I was run down and malnourished from a week-long stomach bug.

I have no rational reason to hate Mariah.

But she is too perfect. She's a good runner, an above-average student, and manages it all while staying out of the gossip.

And then there's Silas. She even snagged him as her boyfriend—a fact I try to forget while I'm left with my own mediocrity. The thought of him is a sharp stitch in my side, worse than any runner's cramp.

"I didn't let you choose your partners, but I suppose I'll let you decide who wears the blindfold," Coach Vance grins, clearly pleased with his joke.

"Do you want to wear it, or should I?" Mariah asks, the politeness so perfectly her.

"I'll wear the blindfold," I say, snatching the cloth from her hand. I don't tell Mariah, but the reason was simple: I'd rather not be yelling out her name, drawing attention to myself. I am more comfortable behind the mask than the center of attention.

Coach places those of us with the blindfold on a line. After a few minutes of waiting, I hear the countdown begin, "Begin in three, two, one. Go!"

Pandemonium erupts—an immediate, high-volume cacophony. Fortunately, we're outside; otherwise, someone would surely mistake the yelling for a murder spree.

"Alexandria!" I hear Mariah's voice in the distance. It is strong and determined. Other girls are screaming the names, high-pitched and frantic. Ashley's voice is piercing, blurring "Casey, Casey, Casey" into one rapid, single-syllable shriek.

At first, it's hard to stay focused. But Mariah is smart; she has a strategy. Her call to me is slow, deep, and deliberate. It reminds me of running—finding a good pace, the perfect tempo paired with the appropriate breathing. She is intentional with the pitch and intonation. I move closer to the sound.

"Alexandria," I hear my name.

Then a pause.

"Alexandria."

It's getting closer.

I bump into something solid. Mariah's summoning ends abruptly followed by a gasp of genuine excitement.

"You can take off your blindfold," she says, her voice still ringing with determination as I free my eyes. "We won," she states, and then without warning, she launches herself toward me and hugs me.

I freeze. My arms stay pinned to my sides, useless and rigid. Every circuit in my brain misfires at the sudden, suffocating proximity. Mariah is all warmth and victory, smelling of floral shampoo and salt, but all I can feel is the hard, clinical edge of her DPU pressing against mine.

Coach Vance blows his whistle, the sound sharp and final. I recoil instantly, stepping back until the air between us is a safe, measurable distance again. "Everyone stop where you are. Take off your blindfold."

He waits for the rest of the team to remove their bandanas. "See where you are in relation to your partner. Congratulations to Mariah and Alexandria for finding each other first."

A scattering of applause follows. It is, I know, mostly for Mariah. Everyone likes her. No one acknowledges my wins, so why would they care about this one?

"Everyone circle up," Coach calls, drawing us to the center of the field. "What did you notice about the last exercise?"

"All I could hear was Ashley, but what else is new?" A wave of chuckles ripples through the team.

I surprise myself by speaking again: "It was all about observation. Mariah heard how everyone else was calling first, and then she made sure her voice was different in tone, pace, and intonation. It stood out, and so it was easier to find her and win."

My own voice sounds like a stranger's. I may be the fastest runner, but I've never been a leader, and I certainly don't volunteer. I seem to have momentarily forgotten my purpose: running for myself, not anyone else. But my mind immediately sees the variable: Mariah's calculated pace and tone. It is pure efficiency—the opposite of my impulsive outburst.

"Exactly, Alexandria," Coach Vance affirms, locking eyes with me. "In the meets, it's no different. We may not be using our voices, but we need to operate within the sixty to eighty percent range and gauge the other runners. You should know your teammates, how they run, their abilities. You've observed each other in practice; now calculate everyone else's moves. Once you've observed, shift your velocity. Your personal efficiency depends on total team compliance." He scans the group huddle looking for confirmation from his players. When he feels it's sufficient, he says, "Think about that. Now, consider yourselves dismissed. See you tomorrow."

Think about that. All I want to think about was a hot shower and four blocks of lonely, purposeful sprint practice. Now, thanks to Coach, even my sanctuary is compromised. I'm not running my own race anymore; I'm being forced to carry the weight of the whole team's efficiency. My pace is no longer my own.

# Chapter 6

His logic is sound, but I hate admitting it. While I despised almost every second of those team-building exercises, I did feel a brief flash of accomplishment when Mariah announced we won. Her unexpected hug and the applause from the team —both jarring—actually felt nice. I rarely feel seen and appreciated.

But I didn't join cross-country to be part of a team. I joined it for me, to get better and improve my personal records. Mostly, I enjoy running, the way it feels, how it helps me escape my reality, both mentally and physically. Yet, Coach made an important point: to truly get better, I must observe and adjust. There's no way to improve if my world is limited to just me; we need to work as a team.

The close proximity leaves me grimier than a typical run. I decide to use the school showers. Very few girls use them, constantly whining about how 'dirty' they look, but it's mostly the dim lighting and the thought of sharing stalls. I don't mind it, and because hardly anyone uses them, there's always warm water—a luxury.

If I wait until I get home, I can barely get a moment in the bathroom without interruption, whether it's the twins calling me to play or Mom needing help with dinner. And getting warm water is a gamble, given how much Kiera uses for the twins' endless bedtime baths. Home is a bizarre setup these days: I either feel completely unseen or in constant demand.

James has been gone for years now.

We see him rarely, usually holidays, and he never comes alone. Brooklyn is always with him—a friend from high school he started dating shortly after moving out. They've been living together in Boston for the last few years.

At first, I thought James needed to escape Lynn, but once he started bringing Brooklyn around, I wondered if he simply needed a break from me. He'd moved on; he'd replaced me with her.

Dad's reputable position at the Testing Center didn't just give him power; it gave the twins a right to exist. Under the Amendment, they should have been 'non-viable surplus'—state property—but his status bought their way into James's old bedroom, and Kiera along with them. Now, we aren't a family; we are a legal obligation, tethered together by a state that forbids divorce until the last child is grown.

It would have been cleaner, simpler, to give the babies up for adoption and pretend the whole affair never happened, since divorce was off-limits anyway.

Instead, my entire world was thrown into upheaval at the age of eleven.

Back then, I was too angry to speak. Mom did more than maintain a facade of normalcy; she went out of her way to be kind to Kiera, the woman who had destroyed our family. She cooked her dinner, ensured all her clothes were clean, and was even at her bedside throughout the entire labor and delivery.

If I didn't understand why they kept the twins, I certainly didn't understand why Mom was so unbelievably nice to Kiera. She could have made her life a living hell.

Anytime I tried to ask Mom about it, I was shut down before I could finish a sentence. Once, early in the new family dynamic, I was helping Mom cook. I portioned out everyone's meal, and when she wasn't looking, I snuck some sour milk and stirred it into Kiera's mashed potatoes. Kiera spent the entire night vomiting. When I woke up, Mom had silently confiscated all my favorite belongings, including my beloved earbuds. I didn't get them back for three weeks. Mom never spoke a word about it; she knew and delivered the punishment.

---

I keep my head down. It's the easiest way. If I stay quiet, no one notices. No one asks. As long as I'm home to chop vegetables or wrangle the twins, no one questions where I've been. Otherwise, I disappear—into homework, into practice, into the safety of Gran and Gramps' house. Anywhere but home.

Charging the DPU is the final chore of the day. The Mandatory Wellness app glows on the phone screen, specifically the cycle tracking—the most annoying requirement for the district's health report. Logging the data feels no different than a boring homework assignment. Numbers are all they want; policy is all that matters.

Halfway to the showers, towel in hand, Ashley's voice cuts through the hallway. Halfway there, Ashley's voice slices out from the equipment closet—sharp, fake-sweet, impossible to miss. My pulse jumps. I reach for the doorknob when a moan leaks through the crack.

Hell no. I yank my hand back, feeling a wave of heat and disgust. The last thing I need burned into my brain is Ashley naked grinding against some desperate kid. Figures—idiots always find a way, law or not. Under the bleachers, in the library bathroom, now the equipment room. This school is basically one big motel.

The shower handle cranks to the limit, unleashing a spray as hot as the pipes allow. Steam swallows me up and for once, I can breathe. At home, five minutes tops—the water's freezing and someone is always banging on the door. But here? I scrub slowly, peppermint body wash stinging my nose, conditioner soaking into my hair while the heat needles my skin. For a few minutes, I almost forget.

Light and sing-songy, chatter starts by the mirrors.

"I heard her dad, mom, and second mommy all sleep together."

Giggles.

"Must be nice to have the government force you into a threesome."

My stomach knots. They're talking about me. I know it.

More laughter, then Ashley again, smooth and cruel: "I heard her mom never put out, so he had to find someone who would."

Casey piles on: "Too bad he got her pregnant, or else he could've had the best of both worlds."

Heat drains out of me faster than the shower. Fourteen and running her mouth like she's some sex expert. I can't take another second.

The familiar burn climbs my throat—the one Gran classifies as a 'marker of instability.' I take a breath, starving the reaction of oxygen. I shut off the water, knot the towel around me, and step out. Proving their profile accurate is no longer an option. My directive is calculated action, not chaos. I'll let them see me. Let them choke on their lip liner.

My hair drips down my shoulders as I stand behind them, silent, waiting. They don't notice me at first. Casey leans so close to the mirror her lashes almost brush the glass, her mouth puckered as she drags the wand over her top lip. Ashley perches on the counter, while the third girl—Madison, maybe—cackles at every word.

The overhead light buzzes. Water drips from my hair, a steady tap-tap-tap on the tile. Still nothing. They're too wrapped up in their own reflections to notice the ghost standing behind them.

I shift my weight on purpose. The squeak of my wet foot against the tile is loud enough to startle them.

Casey's eyes flick up, catching mine in the mirror. Her lipstick stalls mid-swipe.

Ashley notices next. She freezes, mascara wand hovering barely above her lashes. For what feels like the first time today, her voice goes silent.

Good, let them squirm.

I don't move, don't say a word. The towel clings damp and heavy to my skin, but I hold their eyes like I've got all the time in the world. My heart hammers against my ribs, threatening to expel from my chest—but my face remains a mask.

Ashley's mouth curves, but it isn't a smile. More like a dare. She caps her mascara slowly, deliberately, then turns half her body toward me, one eyebrow arched.

"What?" she says, flat and sharp as a blade.

My throat burns with everything I could say. I let out a short laugh. Ashley's smirk deepens, but I don't wait. I shove her—harder than I mean to, maybe, but not enough to knock her down—enough so she stumbles back against the counter with a tiny gasp.

"Don't talk so much shit, or maybe you'll end up with chlamydia or some STD because you can't stop putting out for every dick in the hallway." I push past them, dripping water across the floor like breadcrumbs behind me.

Turning right before I reach the lockers I can't help myself, "And you're fourteen, what do you know about sex? Unless you're as easy as her." I make an exaggerated head move toward Ashley.

My eyes lock on the third girl. The giggle—that calculated, intentional frequency that guided me through the dark just an hour ago—belongs to Mariah.

The air leaves my lungs. I feel my cheeks start to blush, and my heart flutters a little faster. But I don't skip a beat: "And maybe you should stop pretending to be so perfect since you think it's so funny to talk about other people."

At my locker, I still feel the heat in my palms, the rush in my chest. For once, I didn't merely stand there. I committed the exact kind of impulsive, uncalculated chaos Gran and Coach Vance warn against. So much for camaraderie, a common purpose, and behaving like a team.

# Chapter 7

The mile-and-a-half walk home is usually my slow, quiet therapy. I zone out, letting the music's tempo smooth the rough edges of my day while I prepare for the pandemonium of two six-year-olds. As long as I arrive in time to cook, my absence goes unnoticed—it doesn't matter if the walk takes forty minutes or eight. But today is different.

The girls in the locker room hadn't just gossiped about my family; they'd treated our wreckage like a sitcom, finding amusement in my humiliation. Such casual, plain disregard stung more than any whisper ever had. I don't need a cooldown; I need an overdrive. Running is the only therapy available, and today, I need an overdose.

I lace my sneakers so tight the tops of my feet ache. The DPU hums against my hip, a steady reminder of my status. Most students aren't required to wear them—the trackers are a 'privilege' reserved for athletes, the ones the State views as potential high-performance assets. For us, there is no such thing as an unmonitored breath.

Shoving my earbuds in, I crank up DJ Xtra. His mashups—current hip-hop bleeding into Gran's old pop music—are perfect. The erratic tempo gives me an opponent, a challenge to keep my feet aligned with the beat. I start at a focused seventy-five percent effort, but the music and the brisk early-October air demand more. The air feels sharp and clean in my lungs, pushing me toward my maximum velocity.

I settle into the run, trying to shut down my brain, but even with the volume high, I can hear a faint, high-pitched hum—the tiny, incessant digital click of the DPU clipped to my shorts. It isn't loud, but it is always there, a constant monitor of every stride, every breath.

I push harder. Let the metrics show efficiency, not weakness.

The DPU pulses a sharp, rhythmic amber against my hip—a warning that I've exceeded the safe exertion threshold. I ignore it. If the State wants my data, I'll give them a masterpiece of exertion.

As I near my street, I zoom past the turn. I need more time.

My focus isn't on pace; it's on the burn in my lungs, trying to match the physical pain to the swirling questions in my head. I push until the metallic taste of copper coats the back of my throat— the physical toll of a body operating at one hundred percent. My vision blurs at the edges, the world narrowing until all that exists is the rhythm of my feet and the fire in my chest.

Twenty-five. Kiera was twenty-five, a secretary at Dad's office when he got her pregnant. She never had to undergo sterilization. Her only obligation as a female was the benchmarks. She was lucky. Between her diploma, three years of tenure at the Testing Center, and the money she'd saved living at home, she had a head start. The system is all about metrics, and Kiera simply had the right ones at the right time. If she hadn't passed the benchmarks, she would have been denied an option and forced to give the twins up for adoption.

Dad understood the law—he knew the price of infidelity. Was he mindlessly lusting after a younger person and couldn't help it? Did Mom do something wrong?

The mere possibility makes me push harder, my legs churning, but these are thoughts I can't outrun.

And Mom. The way she bends over backward to please Kiera, cooking for her, cleaning up after the product of Dad's blatant disregard for her. She spends her days in the maternity ward holding other people's babies, fully aware of Lynn's whispers—even the new mothers. She should despise Dad and Kiera. My whole body aches with her groundless obedience.

It's hard not to think about how life could have been different. Endless what-if questions consume my mind; I'll never find the answers.

I finish the trail and slow to a jog. Dread weighs down my feet. Mom is likely waiting for my help with dinner, ensuring it's ready by six sharp when Dad walks in.

I finally stop, hands on my knees, chest heaving. The run hasn't settled the chaos; it's only confirmed it. I look at the DPU, flashing faintly on my shorts. I can't control my family, my classmates, or the past, but I can control the metrics.

# Chapter 8

Before Kiera, cooking with Mom was my sanctuary. I'd arrive home, and she'd send James to do his homework. The focus immediately would shift to me. She handed me a list of ingredients—my first task.

While she went upstairs to change, I could almost feel her peeking around the stairwell, ensuring I had every jar, every spice, and every clean utensil lined up on the counter.

She showered me with praise: "Excellent job, Alexandria! You are so organized. You're going to make a great wife and mother."

I once thrived on the praise. I wanted the honor. It's all I dreamed of becoming: to be important enough to carry the responsibility of motherhood under the Twenty-Ninth Amendment.

When she returned, the work began.

I stood on my stool, listening to the rhythm of her voice reading the directions, my hands executing the action. The years melted away: at six, she guided my fingers on the can opener; at eight, she handed me a small, single knife, my first lesson in technique. By nine, I was capable of handling the sharpest blade, trusted to manage the stove's hot, glowing coils.

The kitchen filled with the sizzle of butter and the steady thud of the cutting board.

"You could be a chef," Mom said one afternoon, watching me dice a batch of sweet potatoes. "The efficiency and precision—it's remarkable."

Now, the routine is sterile.

And my dreams of being a mother or a chef have dissipated.

I walk through the door. Mom hasn't waited; all the ingredients are already laid out on the counter next to the recipe. The expectation is silent: Get started.

Before I can even wash my hands, the six-year-old twin whirlwind hits me.

"Alex, you're home! Can you play a game with us?" Charlotte squeals, followed instantly by Savannah.

"Hi Charlotte, hi Savannah," I say, barely looking up as I drop my bag. I should hate them. They are the walking, talking embodiment of my family's ruin. Instead, in small doses, their six-year-old neediness makes me feel seen.

"Why do you say hi to Charlotte first?" Savannah whines, tugging at my shirt.

"Hi Savannah, hi Charlotte," I tease, deliberately swapping my gaze between them as I give Savannah's hair a quick tousle.

Mom comes down the steps, a berry medley in a bowl. She calls out the names, switching the order: "Charlotte, Savannah, come sit and have your snack." I hadn't even heard her on the stairs, but she's heard everything. It's uncanny how much Mom notices when it doesn't involve Dad.

Grabbing a knife from the counter, I attack the vegetables. Tonight: chicken and vegetable stir fry. I start with the broccoli and carrots—the hard work. Then comes the asparagus and onions. I am efficient, almost mechanical. The mushrooms stay. Mom and Kiera can pick through the bowls if they must, but I will not alter the recipe. Within these walls, the kitchen is one of the few places I have some control.

In a separate skillet, I sear Dad's chicken, making a double portion—as always. I despise catering to his whims, doing his bidding without question. He caused this mess, yet he still gets his meat cooked exactly how he wants it. It's exhausting.

As I finish the teriyaki sauce, Mom grabs a fork, blows on the bite, and offers it to her lips. This is where she used to tell me it was perfect. This is where she'd offer me constructive criticism laced with encouragement. Now, she just tastes it. Her expression remains blank, satisfied with the results of my labor, and she immediately begins dishing it out.

Silence.

That's the feedback I get. The kitchen is still, but the silence confirms my invisibility.

Right on time, the front door opens and shuts. Dad walks in.

"Dinner is ready," Mom calls to Kiera, who is in the living room folding laundry. What does she even do all day? Kiera, the woman whose continued employment is folding clothes while I cook dinner.

"This looks delicious," Dad smiles at Mom. He ignores my contribution, but looks my way. "How was school today? Learn anything interesting in History?"

This is the one subject we can share without pretense. Maybe it's the lingering heat from the locker room confrontation, or Mom's silent hour-long slight, but I can't stomach the usual, "It was fine."

I put down my fork. "You should have heard Mr. Everett today. It reminds me so much of Gran and her tangents about history."

Dad actually chuckles, mumbling in the robotic tone I grew up hearing: 'To preserve order, we must keep an accurate account of history.' I smile. For the first time in a long time, it feels like home.

"Mr. Everett even made it seem like he'd been through so much more than us even though—"

"Can we have dessert?" Savannah interrupts.

"I want to watch TV!" Charlotte groans.

Mom stands up, the dirty dishes clanking together as she collects them.

Kiera leans forward. "They're getting restless. Maybe we can finish this conversation later, Alex."

My blood goes instantly cold.

Who is she?

She is not my mother, she is not old enough to be my guardian, and she certainly doesn't have the moral authority to dismiss me. She is an irresponsible older sister who couldn't stop herself from sleeping with a married man. She is a failure of the system, a walking technicality.

I suppress the urge to scream. Instead, I simply push my chair back. I don't storm away. I walk up the stairs, quiet and deliberate, denying everyone the satisfaction of a tantrum.

"But you said you were going to play a game with us!" I ignore Savannah's cry and keep walking.

I stop outside the twins' room, leaning against the door frame. Right now, I'm the one thing holding my parents' marriage together. Once I'm out of the house, Mom is legally able to leave Dad. But watching her act like a slave to him and Kiera, doing laundry and picking mushrooms out of Savannah's food, I find it doubtful she'd ever leave. She'll be trapped, and the girls—my sisters—will grow up thinking this is normal.

This is the ultimate failure of the Twenty-Ninth Amendment. The whole point, the catalyst for the ripple effect—population control, climate stability, economic improvement—was to eliminate kids from broken and unstable homes. The research proves it: those homes create mental health issues, financial instability, and failed future relationships. They made a law to stop this exact kind of dysfunction, and yet, here we are, forced to live a lie. It makes a mockery of the nation's progress.

I long for James, for the ally who abandoned me. He left me with the mess, and my survival now depends on finding a way out of this house.

A straightened spine and a surge of determination point the way toward the bedroom.

My survival relies on a college acceptance letter. I know Silas applied for early acceptance at Boston University. He's smart and a great athlete; a scholarship is guaranteed. My senior teammates are following the same path, and I'm sure Mariah is applying to BU or UMass Boston to be near him.

Four years of tuition might delay the inevitable, but for an average student, the prospect is hollow. There is no passion, no drive, and no desire to endure more classrooms. The need is for something immediate—something solid.

The bedroom door shuts, music swells to drown out the house, and the laptop screen flickers to life.

A search for 'jobs involving history' yields nothing immediate. A second attempt—'physically active jobs'—leads down a list of firefighters and paramedics until a career interest inventory pops up.

Twenty minutes later, the results flash on the screen: Museum Archivist, Police Officer, Military Personnel.

Archivist. I hear Gran's voice in the word—preservation, order. But such rigid structure has trapped me. I dismiss it, focusing on escape.

Police Officer. This fits: a blend of order and exertion. It requires training rather than years of school, and I like the idea of a recurring fitness test to maintain my metrics.

Military Personnel. The possibilities begin to glow. Discipline, duty, problem-solving. These aren't just career skills; they are the survival tactics I've used in this house for years. The idea of being stationed somewhere else, seeing other states, being part of the United States' first defense—it is the perfect combination of physical activity and a more active form of preservation and order.

I have a plan. The best part? I can enlist the minute I have my high school diploma. No more needing anyone. No more permission required.

The door creaks open barely an inch, the slow, soft friction of wood against the frame. Mom slips into the room, carrying a small basket of my folded laundry. She doesn't look at me, but walks straight to the dresser.

"I told you to put these away, Alex." Her voice is hushed, almost flat. "It's better to keep things orderly."

She pauses, her hand resting on the edge of the dresser. Her gaze doesn't flicker toward me; instead, it anchors on the glowing laptop screen.

I realize too late that the word 'military' is there, bright and bold against the dark room. For three agonizing seconds, she is a statue—an unwavering stillness that makes the air in the room feel thin. She doesn't gasp or lecture. She just stares at the screen, her reflection mirroring her blank, unreadable mask.

Then, she simply looks away, as if the life-altering choice I've just made is nothing more than another piece of laundry to be smoothed over.

"Okay, Mom."

She snaps the last drawer shut and without another word slips back out the door.

# Chapter 9

I wake up with a purposeful weight settled in my chest, a feeling I haven't had since I was a kid in the kitchen, desperate for Mom's praise. Today, I'm ready. Less than eight months of school are left. In less than a year, I'll secure the first government benchmark for a successful adult—a high school diploma—and more importantly, I'll be out. Out from under the weight of Mom, Dad, Kiera, and the twins.

Most of my day is spent not in the classroom, but in a haze of future planning. I picture the military: a viable career built on my passions, accumulating the savings required for conception benchmarks. I wouldn't choose to have kids if I wasn't in a stable, long-term relationship, so the two goals rely on each other.

But age twenty-five is a distant milestone; my focus is on the now.

In all my visions of my future, I am alone. I care about my family, but I hate the turmoil they've caused. If I'm honest, I've resigned myself to a future without them. Even Gran—as much as I love her—she is limited by time.

Maybe this is how James felt. He is seven years older and he was closer to the mess than I was. I was the annoying little sister he loved, but he knew I'd hold him back if he stayed. I want to hold his leaving against him, but the older I get, the more I understand the logic behind his escape. Charlotte and Savannah are not enough for me to stay.

But I wonder: will they blame me for leaving them with whatever this house becomes?

I drift through classes, paying enough attention to get by. Today, I'm grateful for my invisibility. I'm not the best student, but I'm quiet. I'm not needy, and I don't talk. Teachers leave me alone. It works to my advantage.

I round the corner between Anatomy and History when Mariah blindsides me.

She stops me, her hand hovering near the DPU on her own waistband. Since we're both on the cross-country team, we're two of the few students in this hall wired directly into the school's biometric grid. Most kids can hide a panic attack; we get an automated warning in our file.

"Alex, can we talk about yesterday?"

I stiffen, resisting the urge to quicken my pace. Mariah—the quiet, focused athlete who dates Silas, the calm, confident star. She's one of the few people I consider a casual acquaintance, precisely because she's never gossiped. Her laughter yesterday, though faint, bothered me more than Ashley or Casey's malice.

My focus remains fixed on the blur of the linoleum floor, a silent signal of dismissal. She doesn't take the hint.

She puts a hand on my shoulder, her touch an immediate violation. "Alex, come on, talk to me. We've known each other since seventh grade. We've been on the same team ever since then," she pleads, tightening her grip slightly.

My mind races. She's right. She's always been civil, if not nice. I didn't actually hear her say anything; I heard her giggle at the cruelty. I pause, forcing myself to process her desperation.

She interprets the silence as permission to explain herself. "The DPU logged a 15-minute spike in heart rate. My parents got an automated letter—they flagged my file with a 'Low Social Assimilation' warning. This cannot be on my record; I'm trying to get a college scholarship."

The irony crushes me. The system monitors heart rate for efficiency, but punishes her for a heart rate spike caused by social stress.

She pulls her hand away, wiping her eyes quickly, then leans in, as if sharing a secret. Then the excuses tumble out of her mouth. "I've never said anything about you, even when I first moved here. People tried to fill me in on the gossip, and I'd stop them. It's not my business. Silas and I talk about it all the time. We get so annoyed with the way people talk because we all have family stuff."

We all have family stuff.

My curiosity curdles into a spike of contempt. How can she compare whatever quiet drama her perfect family has to mine—the pregnant secretary, the twins, the shared roof? Why are she and Silas even discussing me behind closed doors?

She clearly fails to grasp the obvious: the town whispers because my life is a public disaster.

Her mouth keeps moving, driven by a mix of guilt and nervous energy. I'm not used to this much attention, and her words blur.

"I laughed because the joke caught me off guard," she insists. "And sometimes you have to do stuff you wouldn't normally do to fit in. You should try it. You don't make things easy on yourself."

My entire body goes rigid.

The conversation is over.

I didn't ask for any of this. I didn't ask for Dad to cheat. I didn't ask for James to leave me. I didn't ask for Kiera or the twins. I didn't ask for Mom to shut me out. I didn't ask for people to talk shit about me because of something my dad did, not me. I didn't ask to be born. I didn't ask for any of it.

"Sometimes you have to perform compliance to fit in. You should try it. You're making yourself an outlier, Alex. Talk to them more. Maybe then they'd have less to say about you." She digs herself deeper.

She sounds just like Mom. She's advocating for the same groundless obedience that turned my house into a tomb. Mariah isn't offering advice; she's offering a sedative. She wants me to join her in the lie so she doesn't have to feel guilty for laughing at it.

The rage rushes up my throat, choking the breath in my lungs. I pivot, catching her off guard. I slam my palm flat against her shoulder, shoving her hard into the row of lockers. The metal bangs with a sudden, painful sound—a loud, ringing note that echoes down the hallway like an alarm. For a second, the world stops. I've just traded my invisibility for a permanent red flag.

"Stop talking!" I snarl, the sound rough and foreign. "It's obvious you think you're perfect, but you don't know anything about me or my family. So stop pretending you know what's best for me."

I look at her face long enough to see the shock bloom wide in her eyes. Before she can stammer out a response or regain her balance, I feel the familiar burn of instability—the chaos I'm fighting to eliminate— flash through my chest. I turn my back, marching toward History; my pulse is hammering against my skin. I don't need to look down to know my DPU is screaming. If Mariah was flagged for a giggle, I've lit my own file on fire.

# Chapter 10

The adrenaline from shoving Mariah still hums under my skin. I refuse to let her ruin my focus. I pride myself on self-control, on discipline, yet two days in a row, someone has rattled me enough to act impulsively.

What's gotten into me?

A dark thought surfaces: Maybe self-control and suppressing the truth aren't always what's best. I've watched Mom do it for seven years, and look where it's landed her: she manages Kiera's life, guides the woman who slept with her husband through motherhood, and still coddles the man who betrayed her.

After all these years, I've absorbed the lessons from documentaries and Gran's stories: change demands people to speak up. But I always watched from the sidelines, letting everyone else decide what was right, letting Mom and Dad decide the future of our family, letting my classmates talk.

The passivity stops now. I am in control of my destiny.

Despite the confrontation, I'm fired up, eager to go to History. Mariah's rage-fueled comment has sharpened my mind for debate. I can't wait to hear the presentations, and I'm hungry to see how Mr. Everett will stir controversy while holding fast to his patriotic reverence.

Normally I claim my seat early, but the Mariah debacle slows me. I walk in as the bell shrieks. Cody is sitting at my desk, the one by the window. We don't have assigned seats, but the seating arrangement is an unspoken, sacred contract.

I see him next to Melody and instantly understand. He's had a crush on her since elementary school. Why he's trying now, senior year, is a mystery —he's wasted too much time for any real chance. He shouldn't be messing with the higher order of unassigned assigned seats.

There is one open spot in the back next to Silas, where Cody normally sits. Mr. Everett's gaze tracks me, a silent pressure pushing me into the open chair. I slide into the seat next to Silas, the air around him buzzing with a restless, defiant energy that makes the back of my neck prickle.

Sitting next to Silas, I wonder if the system can sense the friction between us—the girl who just committed assault in the hallway sitting next to the boy who looks like he's ready to set the mural on fire.

If I could lower my heart rate, I could erase the evidence of the shove. I force a slow, deep breath, watching for the indicator light to settle.

Mr. Everett opens class, stabbing a yardstick against the board where 'Twenty-Ninth Amendment' is written. He hits the board a little too forcefully. "Who can recite the Twenty-Ninth Amendment?"

Reciting it by memory is the History equivalent of multiplication tables—it's drilled into our bones. Even though it's written on the muraled wall, no one needs to look at it. I think about how often we're told: "Our country is still standing because of the Twenty-Ninth Amendment." I truly am grateful to live in this stable time, far from the shambles Gran's parents described.

No one raises a hand. "Come on," Mr. Everett says, frustration etching his voice. "You've been doing this since you were six. Don't make me have you all come up here and say it."

A few people sacrifice themselves for the common good. Cody stands, his voice immediately shifting into a too-professional cadence: "The Twenty-Ninth Amendment states: The right of citizens of the United States to procreate and/or raise children, will begin at twenty-five years of age or older."

I look around. The vast majority of people are mouthing the words instinctively, their lips moving with Cody's robotic recitation. "The citizens must meet the financial threshold, intelligence quotient, and relational status qualifications requisite determined by each State. The Congress shall have power to enforce this article by appropriate legislation."

Everyone's lips stop with his final, stiff sentence.

"Thank you, Cody. Today, and throughout next week, you will hear a lot about cause and effect. Ultimately, all of these matters have undoubtedly been impacted by the Twenty-Ninth Amendment. First up today, we will be hearing from Melody."

Melody, normally shy, shifts nervously but gathers her materials. As she starts talking, her voice finds a confident, even monotone. She speaks as if looking right through us, focusing on how the Amendment resulted in population control and its impact on the environment.

"When President Wolf was elected in 2028, the United States had been the leading country in emitting carbon dioxide from fossil fuels for hundreds of years..."

Melody outlines the benefits of decreased population and a smaller carbon footprint. She presents decent points, but her logic is flawed. She uses too many generalities and fails to delve into other factors.

I want to jump in. Mr. Everett should address this. It's important to understand the complexities; the Amendment isn't the only factor in sustainability. I have nothing against Melody, but her presentation is missing facts, and worse, it's missing passion.

The class gives a scattered, unenthused applause. I join, the rhythm practiced since elementary school—it's less about respect for the speaker and more about reverence for the subject. Failing to applaud is a red flag, signaling ungratefulness, or worse, rebellion.

"Thank you, Melody. We will have two more presentations. But first, we will recite the Twenty-Ninth Amendment. Do I have a volunteer this time, or do we all need to do it?"

To my surprise, Silas raises his hand. He recites the Amendment flawlessly but his tone is entirely different from Cody's. It's derisive, almost mocking. It's a quiet rebellion, something I wouldn't dare to do. If Mr. Everett notices, he ignores it, focused on moving along. "Thank you for your precision, Mr.

Wright," he acknowledges, then continues.. "Next up is Cody, followed by Austin."

Cody gives a mediocre presentation on the economy. Valid points, but his delivery is monotone and stiff. My enthusiasm for class dwindles. I suspect Mr. Everett purposefully scheduled the weaker speakers first, saving the best for later. I cling to the hope that this week won't be a total loss.

Once Cody finishes, the applause is obviously obligatory. "We will finish today with Austin. Come on up."

Austin, a nerdy kid who moved from Vermont at the start of high school, steps forward. I brace myself. His presentations are usually concise, informative, and compelling. He doesn't have an arrogant confidence, but he knows his subject, and he commands the room without demanding attention.

"Before the Twenty-Ninth Amendment, educators were expected to take on the roles of many different careers: not only teacher but nurse, therapist, babysitter, parent, entertainer, and custodian. The list goes on," Austin begins. "Their responsibilities were magnified, but student expectations diminished. There was no accountability for children who were able to behave however they wanted without consequence at school or home."

"Teachers were forced to pass students along to the next grade or provide them with a minimum score even if the child chose not to complete work. Educators had to sit through hours of training where they were told how they could improve their methods to better meet the needs of students. Every year, the expectation would change: 'technology is efficient and the way of the twenty-first century,' and then five years later, 'technology is addictive and hindering basic skills and retention.' Education lacked consistency, save for a single rule: teachers bore the responsibility to meet a child's needs using any measure or method required."

He shares the old stories—Columbine, Sandy Hook—tragedies we can barely imagine. We respect our teachers because we know our education is invaluable, a foundation for success, a requirement for the Twenty-Ninth Amendment's benchmark of a productive citizen. It's hard to imagine what life was like when this was not the standard.

"Some argued removing reproductive choice was a breach of the unalienable rights to life, liberty, and the pursuit of happiness," Austin continues. "But after years of deliberation, the verdict held: the choice to bear children often impeded a child's own inalienable rights, especially if they weren't provided for properly."

His argument echoes my exact thoughts from minutes ago. He sees the truth I live with every day. I didn't ask to be born into this. When left to their own devices, people make selfish decisions. Such behavior is the reason laws exist. President Wolf realized excessive freedoms hindered the rights of the vulnerable. The Twenty-Ninth Amendment wasn't a choice—it served as a mandatory correction for a failing society.

It feels like Austin is reading my mind: "The requirements set by the Twenty-Ninth Amendment don't prevent one-hundred percent of these problems, but they certainly deter. Someone truly has to be intentional about having children. There is no initial accident. There are two stable parents, each at a fully developed age, involved in a child's life..."

He details the benchmarks: financial security, education, a consistent job—metrics ensuring a child doesn't suffer, standards to instill discipline and stability. "The Twenty-Ninth Amendment guarantees this," he concludes.

The class erupts in applause, and I join in, my hands hitting together with enthusiasm. I glance over at Silas. He doesn't seem as enamored as everyone else. He has a tight, unreadable look, but I push the observation away. Austin's words reinforce my conviction.

I have a greater purpose than cooking dinner or winning a cross-country banner. Serving in the military is the ultimate way to protect what my ancestors fought for. It's a way to preserve this ordered history and prevent other children from suffering the way I do. The Twenty-Ninth Amendment made things immeasurably better, but the work remains—work I intend to finish.

# Chapter 11

An adrenaline spike from History still pulses in my veins. A Friday ending in renewed purpose and a home meet is a rare win. The day is a collection of my favorite things. No day is perfect, so I'm focused on the good. Tonight, I'll be with Gran and Gramps.

On my way to the locker room, I brace myself for the sight of Ashley, Casey, and Mariah. The last twenty-four hours have been a whirlwind of outbursts and confrontation, but now, preoccupied with Austin's speech and my military purpose, the dread is duller. Mariah is still an idiot for what she said, but at least she delivered the final blow to my face.

The usual locker room chatter dies the instant they register my presence. The silence is a punch. They are all standing there, frozen mid-motion, indifferent stages of undress. It's almost comical: Ashley is exposed in a sports bra, Mariah has her shorts halfway up her thighs, and Casey's hands are tangled in her ponytail.

I don't give them the satisfaction of a prolonged glance. I walk straight to my locker. The loud reverberation of chatter is gone, replaced by a sudden, stale tension. Now, I can hear every little move, every squeak of a shoe, every rasp of fabric.

On a typical game day, the air is thick with nervousness and competitive energy. Now, the tension is a solid wall.

Just yesterday, Coach Vance spent practice chewing us out for not behaving like a team, forcing us through ridiculous team-building drills. For a second, it felt like it worked. Now, look at us.

Normally I'm invisible, but today, I am the center of a silent, rigid audience. Before yesterday, I was predictable. I would have ignored their whispers and hidden in the shower until the locker room cleared. Now, my reaction is an unknown variable. They wonder if I'll still choose the path of least resistance with Mariah. But after the last twenty-four hours, my silence is no longer a guarantee of safety.

I could make this easy. I am the source of tension, whether I asked for it or not. If I dropped, they'd be relieved—quick apologies, a side-hug, and the gossip would be forgotten for the time being.

My pride wants to be stubborn. I want them to wallow in the guilt, not merely for yesterday, but for what I've carried for so long. How hard is it for them to feel an ounce of the shame I endure every day? But another part of me wants to be agreeable. I hate disappointing Coach Vance and the team. Tension sinks our performance.

I can't be docile or compliant for the sake of others anymore. I'm done mimicking Mom's choice to accommodate everyone but herself. But in this case, alleviating the tension is what's best for the team. There has to be a middle ground. My greater purpose sometimes means speaking up, even when I don't want to.

The metal-on-metal clang of my locker door is the final period to their silence. I turn to face them.

"Don't stop talking on my account. It never stopped you before." My voice is low and sharp, intended to sting.

I deliver the lines Coach Vance wants to hear, using the same rehearsed tone my father uses when he's lying to Mom.

"We have a meet to win. Success requires us to work together, a goal far more important than any gossip you think you know about my life." I throw one final sliver of shade. If they can talk behind my back, I can do it to their faces. "What do you say? Ready to work together rather than against each other?"

Heads nod, and a few verbal grunts break the silence.

It works.

The tension in the room doesn't disappear; it just realigns into a productive shape. I'm finally learning how to be a performance artist.

Catching Mariah's eye, she mouths, "Thank you."

I acknowledge her with the slightest dip of my head. I haven't truly forgiven her, but I'm ready to drop it.

Outside, Coach calls us into a tight huddle, breaking down the game plan for the course. "Look to Alex for the velocity change. Most importantly, communicate," he commands, thrusting his hand into the center.

We follow his lead, palms stacking one on top of the other. Mariah takes charge, shouting, "1, 2, 3," and we all yell in unison, "Rams."

Our home course is shy of five miles. I have a knack for endurance, a rhythm outlasting runners who can't pace themselves. I know the course, and I know those first chaotic hundred meters are always a scramble.

The starter's gun cracks—and the pandemonium begins.

I surge forward, pushing through the initial cluster, focusing on settling into my stride. I am running at about seventy-five percent effort. This is a longer course, and I need the reserve. Mariah is right behind me, the others not too far from her. Coach has entrusted me to win, but to also lead by example. They'll use my shift in velocity as their gauge.

I glide past the underclassmen who shot out too quickly. As we round the bend before the two-mile mark, I pore more effort into my legs, smoothly increasing my velocity. I take a quick look back to confirm the signal. Mariah catches my eye and relays the signal to the runners behind her with a curt nod. This is the biggest shift in this run. For the next two miles, I can zone out, moving with the sound of my feet hitting the ground. My heart races, my arms pump. There is no better feeling.

In almost no time, I hit the final stretch. I push to my maximum speed. I don't dare to turn my head, but I don't hear anyone nearby either. The roar of the crowd is a physical force now, pulling me toward the finish line.

At 25.44, I cross the finish line and immediately slow to a jog. I can't stop moving, or the pain will seize me tomorrow. I jog backward, watching the rest of the runners funnel through the finish.

Our rival brings in the second runner almost a full minute later at 26.32. Mariah is right behind her at 26.55, one of her best times. She slows to a jog and her face, sweaty and exhausted, breaks into a smile.

Instead of cooling down near me, she makes her way toward the stands. I see a flash of black hair and then Silas rushing toward her. He meets her halfway, picking her up in a powerful and engulfing hug. Mariah bends her legs at the knees, letting him lift her off the ground and swing her in a wide arc.

It's jarring.

I rarely see Silas happy. He's usually unruffled, difficult to read, combative in History. I've never seen him smile like this. Mariah is good at everything and she elicits pure, unbridled joy from a boy who usually gives nothing. She really does have it all.

A wave of sweat-drenched arms collapses around me. Casey, Ashley, and the rest of the team are closing in, dragging me back to reality. The fans are cheering incessantly; I can't hear anything over the sound. I am engulfed in a frantic, sweaty group hug, jumping up and down with the rest of them.

Of the top ten finishes, six are ours. We won by a landslide.

While the team screams and jumps around me, the cold vibration against my hip is the only thing that feels real—a notification that I've hit my peak performance metrics. It's the only congratulations I actually trust. The team's praise is fickle—driven by the high of a win—but the DPU is objective. It doesn't care if I'm a 'blight' or if my dad is a cheat; it only knows I am efficient. I am an asset.

Coach Vance clears his voice, cutting through the celebratory roar: "Seems our team-building actually paid off! Excellent communication today, team!"

Communication, discipline, winning. This is what I can control. This is the viable pathway to the military, a better form of order than the one I live in.

# Chapter 12

I should be euphoric. We scored a crushing win, and I actually took control in the locker room. But the high has already evaporated, replaced by a hollow emptiness. I wish I had someone to talk to, but my well of trust is dry. I'm so used to being the subject of gossip I've never let anyone in—not even the nice ones.

Dad and Mom are buried in the logistics of their work, leaving me with a mother who prefers the safety of silent judgment to an actual conversation. The twins are just high-maintenance variables I can't solve. Then there's Kiera—the catalyst for every fracture in this foundation—and James, who performed the ultimate calculation and simply subtracted himself from the house entirely.

Since the affair became public, an unspoken strain has settled between Mom and Gran. They are still civil, kind even, but their mannerisms suggest differently. Their movements around each other are stiff like dry, brittle wood. Our weekly dinners dwindled until I realized Mom has used the tradition as one of her few, silent power plays against Dad. When the visits stopped entirely, I started going on my own. Gran always greeted me as if she had expected me. Now it's the three of us, with Gramps acting as a benevolent fixture while Gran and I dominate the space.

The quickest route is four blocks right past our house. I tack on an extra quarter mile to avoid the sight of it. After a meet, I need a slow jog to flush the lactic acid; otherwise, the next day is misery. I jam my earbuds in, starting the two-mile route, trying to lose myself in the music and the pounding of my feet on the asphalt. This is my therapy. I don't need people; I need air and earth.

A mile in, my thoughts race faster than my legs, and my pacing is shot. The ritual isn't working.

I slow to a walk, the rhythmic data of my feet hitting the pavement no longer enough to overwrite the mental noise. My pacing is shot. I squat low on the curb, pulling out my earbuds, and the sudden silence of the street is deafening. I take a jagged breath, trying to settle the frantic, vibrating energy in my chest.

I stop at the corner of Congress and Boston, forcing my eyes off the cracked pavement and up at the architecture. I stand and force myself to look at Lynn, truly look at it, without the lens of my own misery. For as long as I can remember, I've weaponized the scenery against myself. I've seen these old, dilapidated buildings as nothing more than hollow containers for the people who whisper about my father. I've turned Lynn into a backdrop for a scandal that wasn't even mine to carry.

The truth doesn't hit me faintly; it collides with me: I have allowed my family's wreckage to colonize my entire perspective. I've let one terrible, systemic failure—my father's choices—poison the very ground I walk on. I try to unsee the rumors, to find a version of this town that doesn't belong to a secretary or a shared roof.

My chest is heaving, and for a second, the pressure behind my eyes is so heavy it feels like my skull might crack. I hate it. I hate the way my throat tightens, making it hard to swallow, a physical warning that the walls I've built are starting to leak.

I've spent seven years perfecting my armor, and I'm not about to let it dissolve on a random street corner in Lynn. Crying feels like an admission of defeat—a white flag I refuse to wave. I take a jagged breath, forcing the heat in my eyes to cool, pushing the grief back down into that dark pit in my stomach where I keep the rest of my secrets.

I aggressively wipe my face on my sleeve, my skin stinging from the salt and the cold. I don't have time for a system failure. I take one deep, steadying breath, realigning my mask until it feels heavy and secure. Then, I turn the corner and push through Gran's front door.

The living room is dimly lit. Gramps is already asleep in his chair, the television murmuring softly in front of him. Gran meets me at the threshold instantly. She wraps an arm around my shoulders, drawing me into the warm scent of her sweater.

"I know I'm no chef like you, but I made your favorite." The scent of sweet batter is already reaching me. French toast, eggs, and sausage– breakfast for dinner, my comfort food.

As we walk into the kitchen, I take my seat. Gran starts dishing out the food from the stove, calling out loudly, "Eugene, dinner's ready!" She lowers her voice, murmuring to me, "I'll have to go in there and wake him. You know how—" She pauses mid-sentence as she turns, bringing the heavy plates to the table. "Alexandria, what's wrong? Have you been crying?"

I wipe my eyes self-consciously. "No, am I red? It's really cold out, and I was running against the wind," I stumble, hearing the unconvincing lie hang in the air.

Gran is the person I'm closest to, yet the old hesitancy and fear rush back. We see each other weekly, we talk history, but we never talk about feelings. Sharing emotions is not a thing our family does, and despite my fondness for her, vulnerability feels like a betrayal.

She sets the plate in front of me and slides into her chair directly across the table. "Forget about Gramps. Let us girls eat together."

"You know breakfast for dinner is my favorite," I say, chewing a bite of French toast, desperate to steer the conversation back to safety.

Then Gran asks, "Tell me, how are things at home?"

I swallow hard. "Gran, you don't need to ask me about home. Let's do what we normally do. Tell me one of your stories. Let's watch a documentary."

"Then let me tell you a short story about the more recent past," she gives a subtle, knowing smile, "about you."

Butterflies erupt in my stomach. It's nice to be seen, but to be the center of attention is instant anxiety.

"Do you know why we named you Alexandria?" she asks.

The word choice 'we' throws me off. I look at her expectantly.

"Your name, Alexandria, means 'defender of the people'—a heavy responsibility. True defense, darling, is not messy or emotional. You are meant to be a clear signal in a world of noise You are meant to rise above the chaos and regulate it. Don't forget it."

I chew a piece of sausage, letting the weight of my name sink in. The thought behind it surprises me, and I'm suddenly curious why Dad was named Lincoln or why James was named after Jamestown.

Gran waves her hand dismissively. "But maybe we've been focusing too much on the past and not enough on the present. How about we start talking about the present?"

I can't remember a time that anyone has asked me to talk about my feelings. I've been swallowing my emotions for the last seven years. They've been sitting in the pit of my stomach, ruminating, waiting to be released. As much as I want to purge them, I can't.

I counter, "How about we start by talking about the future?"

As Gramps snores lightly from the living room, I lay out my three career ideas. Gran listens, genuinely interested. When I mention the museum archivist, she recites her old Gran-ism: "To preserve order, we must keep an accurate account of history." She is even more excited about the police force and the military. Her enthusiasm rouses a delight I haven't felt since those early days in the kitchen with Mom. An adult is taking a sincere interest in my goals, validating my abilities and my purpose.

The more we talk about my future, the more relaxed I become. The topic shifts naturally to my family, and this time, I let it. Gran isn't an outsider; she knows most of it, and she won't spread rumors because the scandal touches her reputation, too.

"I know it hasn't been easy since Kiera and the girls became part of the picture," Gran says gently. "But your Dad tried to do what was right by everyone."

Everyone? I swallow the protest, knowing she's a mother defending her son.

I respond hesitantly, "I wish he had considered the consequences before getting himself into this situation."

Gran nods in agreement. "Prevention would have been preferable, but men are men. Human nature is exactly why the Twenty-Ninth Amendment passed. By providing legal boundaries and ramifications, it drastically improved the situation, but the unprecedented can still happen—like with your dad and Kiera."

"I don't understand why Dad was given a choice," I insist. "The law exists for a reason, and the twins should have been placed for adoption. It shouldn't be a gray area. Massachusetts' law should have been applied fairly."

Gran takes a long moment to consider. "The law exists for a reason, but it's not as black and white as you may think. Your dad is a good man, and he made a mistake—a mistake he may not have made had your mom been a more attentive wife."

The words are a sudden, sharp crack in my sanctuary. Gran has never spoken ill of Mom in front of me. I've never heard her use the 'boys will be boys' mentality, a phrase I thought the Twenty-Ninth Amendment had eliminated. Gran is rewriting the data of my childhood to fit a narrative that keeps her son innocent. It's a logic error I can't ignore. In just a few sentences, my Gran, my safe space has splintered.

"Because of his longevity to the cause at the Testing Center and our family's long line of history fighting for a better America, more grace was given," she explains. "Your dad has paid his debts in other ways."

I am speechless. Everything she has ever preached is about upholding the law, being a productive and upstanding citizen. Now she's defending Dad's hypocrisy and, worse, she's blaming Mom. If I am the 'Defender,' who am I defending now? The man who broke the law, or the mother who was erased by it? Gran doesn't want a defender; she wants a co-conspirator.

I feel a vibration against my hip—my DPU registering the spike in my cortisol. Even here, at this table, the machine knows I'm no longer at peace. There is nowhere left to hide from the data. I am meant to rise above the chaos and regulate it. But sitting here, I realize Gran doesn't want me to regulate the chaos; she wants me to ignore the parts of it that make her uncomfortable.

A heavy lump lodges in my throat, suffocating me. There's so much I want to scream, but my thoughts are an indiscernible noise. I default to the solitary response I can manage: "I guess that makes sense."

I swallow the last bite of French toast. It's cold now, the congealed syrup sticking to the roof of my mouth like lead. The scent of sweet batter, which felt like a hug minutes ago, now smells like a bribe. The breakfast-for-dinner ritual hasn't settled the chaos; it's just provided a better-lit stage for the hypocrisy.

# Chapter 13

I'm actually looking forward to school. Home has become a blur of shared silences with Mom and twins' endless complaints. I spend my nights behind earbuds, drowning it all out. Even Gran's house isn't the escape it used to be—tainted by her 'men will be men' philosophy.

Lost in my thoughts, I'm moving slower than usual. I prefer efficiency: throwing on a T-shirt, a zip-up hoodie, shorts with joggers over top for the coming cold spell. I pull my hair into a ponytail, sling my backpack over my shoulder, and jog down the steps toward the kitchen to make a quick sandwich.

Mom is already at the counter, in her scrubs, assembling the twins' lunches before she heads to the maternity ward. It's absurd—Kiera doesn't work and could be doing this for her own daughters, but Mom takes care of it. I nod back with as little emotion as possible and walk toward the cabinets.

To my surprise, she holds out a brown paper lunch bag. "I noticed you were running late."

"Uh, thanks, Mom. Have a good day." I am utterly stunned.

I hold the brown paper bag like it's a peace treaty I never signed. In this house, kindness is rarely about love. What did I do to deserve a packed lunch and a verbal acknowledgement? It's unnerving. It feels like a bribe for my compliance.

The day flies by. I use every free minute to rehearse my presentation. I'm scheduled to speak today. History is the only class I care about this much, but public speaking makes my hands sweat, so over-preparation is my defense. My topic is how the Twenty-Ninth Amendment improved financial stability. Though I have statistics, I plan to use ethos—the moral argument—as my main appeal.

My conviction is rooted in Gran's stories, which she's shared more openly since I turned eleven. She described a childhood lived in poverty, a time when her grandfather, Ryan, who in addition to having four different kids with three different women, didn't support two of his kids whatsoever, emotionally or financially.

My great-grandmother, Lizzy, never had the chance to meet her two half-siblings. She got a glimpse of her half-brother once. When Lizzy was seven, she was playing outside when a rundown car sputtered onto their unpaved property. A woman emerged, screaming, "Ryan, get out here! I know you're in there. I can see your face all over this little girl's."

When silence met her scream, the woman started throwing rocks and dirt toward the house. "Ryan, you piece of shit. You're over here having more kids and you can't even afford the ones you already have."

Lizzy hid behind the woodpile, peeking out just as a boy, about nine poked his head out of the car window. Their eyes met, before his mother hurled a letter at the front door: "Wait until you're served. I'll take you for all you have." Lizzy never saw her half-brother again.

Even though Lizzy and her brother David lived with their dad, they didn't have it easy. He verbally and physically abused their mother, but she stayed, terrified he'd use her low income to take the children away. Lizzy and David grew up on constant alert, watching their own backs. There wasn't always enough money for groceries; they went to school in torn, outgrown clothes. Lizzy started working at fourteen in order to buy necessities and bring home kitchen leftovers for her brother.

This became their purpose. Lizzy married young, to the older man who owned the restaurant. He later became involved in politics. This connection is how Lizzy, and eventually her brother David, became so involved in the work behind the Twenty-Ninth Amendment. Lizzy's husband used their harrowing story as leverage to persuade leaders that government intervention was the way to break the cycle of abuse and poverty.

Gran talks about Lizzy and David like they were superheroes or the Founding Fathers, their lives a prime example why the Amendment was instituted: to ensure low-lives like Ryan couldn't reproduce and neglect their children. The Amendment puts laws in place so anyone who procreates can provide financial stability, making the decision intentional.

I'm nervous about sharing this history. They already whisper about my family; this feels like adding fuel to the fire. But I decided to make change. Speaking up is the only way. Mr. Everett said it last week: to preserve the good we have, we must remember the suffering of those who came before us.

I've run through my speech enough times to feel ready but Mr. Everett is agitated.

"Hopefully, you didn't forget thirteen years of education over the weekend. Let's start by reciting the Twenty-Ninth Amendment." He doesn't ask for a volunteer. He raises his arms like a conductor, signaling the whole class to begin the robotic chant.

"We have three more days of projects. Today, the order is Athena, Silas, and Alexandria."

Silas. I freeze. Following Silas, who will likely undermine the entire project, is a nightmare. I'm surprised Mr. Everett is letting him present at all after his recent outburst. I know he'll only detract from my focus.

Athena starts. Of course, she begins with an excess of pretension and snobbery. "As I'm sure you know, my parents work for the Lynn municipality. Our family roots run deep. My ancestors helped build this city's legacy as the 'Shoe Capital of the World.' Now, my parents carry the torch, dedicated to making Lynn, and America, the best they can be." She throws in her usual boast: "They collect data supporting the Twenty-Ninth Amendment...hence why they named me 'wisdom.'"

"The numbers show a drastic improvement in the average American intelligence quotient since the Twenty-Ninth Amendment's establishment in 2036," she drones.

Her ostentatiousness repulses me. I tune her out, running my own speech inwardly.

A few minutes later, scattered applause jolts me back.

"Thank you, Athena, for your well-informed presentation. You are all truly fortunate to live in a time with a government looking out for your best interests," Mr. Everett states, as if he isn't trapped in this century with the rest of us.

"Mr. Wright," he pauses. "Are you ready to present?"

Silas stands up, pushing one side of his long hair behind his ear, exposing his lean, strong profile. "Yes, sir, looking forward to it," he replies, stone-faced.

"We've heard some compelling arguments," Silas begins with annoying confidence. He praises Austin's point—the Amendment doesn't completely prevent problems— then pauses for dramatic effect. "But I'm going to bring to the table an unpopular opinion: the benefits don't outweigh the harms."

A few people shift nervously. Mr. Everett doesn't intervene.

"Before the Twenty-Ninth Amendment, the ills of the world were simply more blatant. Now, they're more concealed, hidden from plain sight."

I have never heard anyone speak so openly against the government. Silas is unwavering.

"Austin mentioned people need to be intentional about having children...This may be true, but there are still couples having children who are not emotionally providing for their families. There may be emotional distance in the household, or even worse, undetected verbal or unreported physical abuse. Infidelity or open marriages aren't detected because divorce isn't permissible if there are children under eighteen."

What Mariah said about 'family stuff' flashes back to me. Maybe she wasn't talking about herself. Silas's insights are too specific. He has family drama, too.

"Don't get me started on rabid STI rates among teenagers and young adults who think they're invincible because of sterilization. But I'm sure Athena's parents don't report such data," he says deadpan. Athena looks horrified. The look of offense on her face is worth the rant.

"I'm going to stop you right there, Mr. Wright. There's no reason to make this personal. You're entitled to your opinion, albeit it may be wrong, but you do not need to drag your classmates into it. Go have a seat." Mr. Everett remains surprisingly calm.

"As you wish," Silas surrenders, lifting his hands and moving toward his seat, content with the chaos he sowed.

All of my life, I've been taught how lucky I am to live under these laws. But Silas is making me realize so much gets brushed under the rug. People in power still get away with more, like my dad and Kiera, and it affects those around them.

"Alex, are you ready?"

Shit. I'm startled back to reality. I glance at the DPU clipped to my waistband, its small digital eye a constant witness. Most kids in here can hide their dissent behind a neutral face, but Silas and I are wired into the system. Our bodies tell the truth even when our mouths lie.

"Alex, let's go, you're next," Mr. Everett says impatiently, his irritation now obvious.

I knew Silas would do this.

Standing in front of the class, all eyes on me, I'm flooded with regret. I realize I'm content with being invisible. The classroom is silent, alert, and waiting. The next time I wish someone would notice me, I'm going to remind myself of this moment.

I clear my throat, reciting the rehearsed words. "The Twenty-Ninth Amendment improved financial stability for American families...Many Americans had more children than they could afford to provide for... Others chose to be irresponsible, having children with multiple partners and not necessarily supporting all of their offspring."

I dive into the story. "My great-great-grandfather, Ryan, was like this. He had four children from three different women." Eyes around the classroom grow wide. "Two of his children never lived with him or ever received any type of support... But two of his children did live with him: my great-grandmother Lizzy and her brother David."

I describe the abuse and the poverty. "He was a spendthrift, throwing money away on his car... They often went without food or proper clothing...Lizzy had to get a job at fourteen to help provide."

I describe Ryan's car sputtering onto the property, the screaming woman, the rocks thrown at the door. I'm speaking about the past, but the bile in my throat is purely present-tense. Ryan was a 'low-life' because he couldn't afford his choices. My dad is a 'good man' because he can. The only difference between a historical tragedy and my living room is position.

"This lifestyle turned Lizzy and David into pioneers for the Twenty-Ninth Amendment—ensuring every parent has the financial means and stability to provide. No one should have to undergo what Lizzy, David, and millions of other children had to go through before the government intervened."

The room is filled with wide eyes. They want the tragedy of Great-Great-Grandfather Ryan because he's a safely dead villain. But then I see Silas. He isn't looking at the past; he's looking at me, waiting to see if I'm a coward. The prepared statistics in my head dissolve, replaced by the metallic taste of the truth.

"Thank you, Alexandria," Mr. Everett says, ready to move on.

Before I realize it, I'm interrupting him: "I'm sorry, I'm not done yet though."

A slight irritation flashes across Mr. Everett's face, but he maintains his composure. "No problem. We still have time, so keep going."

"My great-grandparents had a difficult life," I continue, the words tumbling out, unscripted. "Our generation undoubtedly reaps many benefits from the Amendment. But it doesn't mean there aren't problems. What about infidelity?"

The classroom shifts, uncomfortably.

"It may not be something I've talked about before, but all of you have. My dad cheated on my mom and got his mistress pregnant. Because of who he is, he was able to make a decision and keep the children. I may not be starving, but what about the emotional stress inflicted on my family? What about the rules or expectations for my younger half-siblings who have now normalized our family dynamics? What about my mom? She's forced into a marriage with someone who cheated on her because of Lynn's laws. Silas mentioned families experiencing mental or physical abuse. How does the Twenty-Ninth Amendment prevent such trauma? Do we need a benchmark of psychological testing?"

The words start tumbling out like vomit. I didn't plan any of this. I was supposed to stand here and praise the benchmarks, but I'm tired of performing the household script. If the Amendment is supposed to stop trauma, why am I drowning in it?

"Alexandria, we've been through this already. Do you have anything new to add, or is it time to move on?"

"There's more we haven't talked about," I insist, meeting Mr. Everett's eyes. My head is spinning, and new ideas are flooding in. "What about people who want children but are having difficulties conceiving? What about same-sex couples wanting to adopt? Now with population control in effect, there's no longer a surplus of children for people who pass all the benchmarks, but have biological deterrents."

I make eye contact with Silas. He looks directly at me and gives a slight, reassuring nod. I'm not going crazy; these questions require answers.

"It seems to me," I say, my voice steadying even as my DPU burns against my skin, "like maybe instead of moving forward, the Twenty-Ninth Amendment has actually set us back toward the very hierarchy my ancestors fought to dismantle. We've traded one kind of poverty for another. Whether intentional or not, it has caused a disregard and intolerance to those who can't have kids whether due to infertility or sexual—"

"Enough. I've let you go on long enough, Alexandria." His face, usually a mask of academic boredom, has twisted into something sharp and ideological. He doesn't look like a teacher anymore; he looks like a sentry. "This is obscene the way you are blaspheming our government. It is absolutely despicable."

I'm stunned by the severity and harshness of Mr. Everett's words.

"I wasn't trying to—" I stammer.

"I said, enough! Do not continue to speak. Believe me when I say there will be documented consequences for this outburst."

The bell rings, but the students remain frozen in their seats.

"And you too, Mr. Wright. I didn't forget about you and your little stunt. I'll be dealing with both of you later. Go, all of you!"

The DPU at my hip isn't just vibrating anymore; it's a relentless, stinging pulse. Red. I don't have to look to know the light is a frantic, bleeding red. The system is literally recoiling from my words.

# Chapter 14

Any exhilarating rush I felt when standing at the podium vanished the moment I walked out of Mr. Everett's class. I may not be the best student, but I am quiet, the good little girl who flies under the radar. The most common complaint at conferences was 'she needs to put in more effort.' I have never been in trouble at school.

This isn't a minor offense. Depending on how Mr. Everett frames it, my outburst qualifies as an act of disloyalty to the United States, requiring the school to officially report it. What was I thinking?

I wasn't, and therein lies the problem. Everything I said is true, but it doesn't mean I had to scream it into the face of authority.

I still have cross-country practice, and I desperately need it. My whole body is rigid, screaming for release. I know the rhythm of my feet on the pavement will be a release, a necessary purge.

I walk into the locker room, and the chatter is loud, vibrating off the metal lockers. No one sees me enter.

"I heard she stood up to Mr. Everett," Casey's voice cuts through the noise.

"Well, rumor has it she denounced the Twenty-Ninth Amendment as an abomination. A bold statement," Ashley counters.

They aren't even in my class. How does word spread so fast, and why does it get so distorted?

"Silas is organizing a rebellion," another voice says from the other side of the lockers. "Maybe Alex is working with him."

I start changing, ignoring the comments. I'm so used to being talked about. The value of my newfound commitment to truth and confidence is collapsing. Integrity felt empowering until I realized the consequences could be severe. So much for preserving the truth.

Gran was right: too much of anything, even the truth, isn't good.

The gravity of Mr. Everett's threat makes this pathetic rumor mill insignificant.

"Oh stop, Silas is doing nothing of the sort," Mariah says, her voice snapping with impatience. "He's trying to get people to think for themselves rather than believe everything they're told." She is defending him.

"Oh, are you worried, Mariah?" Alicia's teasing voice is designed to needle.

"What are you talking about?" Mariah challenges, instantly defensive.

"Silas will forget all about you now because he's seen a shared passion for treachery inside Alex. Maybe he'll leave you out of his plans and invite his new buddy instead. I'm sure Alex would love to join him," Alicia chuckles.

"That's ridiculous, like everything else you've all been saying. As for Alex, why don't we ask her since she's standing right there." Finally, someone is using some logic. Mariah swings around and looks directly at me, "Alex, is it true? Did you really defy Mr. Everett?"

After our last two clashes, I'm caught off guard by her directness. I'm still pissed at her for laughing at Ashley's joke and for blaming me for the stupidity of others, but I admire her boldness.

"It's not really like that," I manage to stutter.

"So what happened?" Alicia barges into the conversation.

"I was just giving my presentation."

"My information says otherwise. I heard you were bashing our government and the Twenty-Ninth Amendment," Alicia snaps back.

I look from Mariah to Alicia. The 'logic' I hoped for is nowhere to be found. They aren't looking for the truth; they're looking for blood. I feel the DPU vibrate —three sharp pulses—reminding me that every second my heart rate stays elevated, the 'noise' is being quantified as a threat.

The aggression in her voice makes me want to lash out, but I lock it down. I can't risk another impulsive move. If the school reports the class outburst, they'll start digging into my recent encounters—interviewing people, looking for patterns. I haven't been doing myself any favors lately, and I know how quickly people here will exaggerate and fabricate.

I tread lightly, "I was doing the assignment. I wanted to do it justice, present both sides, talk about both the positive and negative aspects." I can't believe I'm explaining myself to her.

"You realize you've entered dangerous territory, don't you, Alex? You have to be careful with what you say." There's an unexpected concern in Mariah's voice.

I'm about to say something when Coach Vance leans in. "Let's go, practice is starting, and I have no runners."

Coach seems more jovial, probably riding the high of the win. We get praise and clichés: You are really working as a team; the team-building really improved our communication; and I knew you could all be leaders. Everyone smiles and thanks him. I'd rather not listen to him, but it beats team-building exercises or lectures.

I am grateful when he leaves us to our own devices to simply run the course. Monotony is exactly what I need. I don't need to pay attention; I know every curve and incline. I zone out for nearly five miles, letting my thoughts scatter.

As I run, my heart rate finally levels into a rhythmic, sanctioned pace. I watch the DPU light fade from a frantic red back to a compliant green, as if the miles can outrun my treason.

The green light is a lie, a false certificate of health. I'm not 'compliant'; I'm just exhausted. The system thinks I'm regulated, but I've just learned how to pace my pulse so it doesn't give me away.

I must be slower than I realize, because some of my teammates begin to pass me. Normally, my pride would flare, forcing me to sprint and beat them, even in practice. But today, I'm empty. My stomach is full of fluttering dread, and I feel weak thinking about the consequences Mr. Everett promised.

Everyone passes me. I'm about a quarter mile from the finish line when I see Mariah running back towards me. She catches up and turns, matching my pace.

"Aren't you done? Why'd you come back?" I ask.

"I know I messed up. I know we're not really friends, but I really admire you, Alex."

I stay silent, trying to hide my perplexed look in the dimming light of the setting sun.

She takes my silence as a cue to continue. "Ever since I moved here, I've envied your confidence. People gossip and talk about you, but you remain poker-faced. It's like it doesn't bother you. Between your stoicism and your running abilities, I've always been jealous."

She doesn't realize I'm stone-faced because if I let a single crack show, the whole foundation will give way. Her jealousy is a misunderstanding of my survival tactics. I'm not 'confident'; I'm just very, very good at hiding.

I still don't speak. After today, I've decided my safest option is to retreat into my shell and stop myself a target.

"Anyway, I came back to tell you I'm sorry about the other day," she rushes out as we near the finish. "But also, you really should be careful. I tell Silas this all the time: it's not your responsibility to change the world. You don't have to agree with everything the government says, but is it worth putting yourself on the line? Be careful is all I'm trying to say."

I don't have time to respond. We close in on the finish line, and I see four shadowed figures joining Coach Vance in the dusk. Even in the dimming light, I recognize my parents' outlines.

"Alexandria, go pack up your things. We've met with Mr. Everett, and we have a lot to discuss."

The group comes into full view. Mom, Dad, Mr. Everett, and—why is Gran here? The four of them stand as a united front—a terrifying alliance I haven't witnessed in years. Mariah pats me on the back and quickly jogs away toward the security of the locker room, leaving me alone to face the aftermath of my decisions.

# Chapter 15

Dad speeds away from the school, leaving behind any exhilaration I felt today, replacing it with a cold fear.

"You're in your last year of school. You seriously couldn't wait eight more months to decide to act out like this?" Dad rarely speaks to me at all, but now he thinks he has the right to blast me like a child. "This could have been absolutely devastating for our family. You don't know how lucky you are—your grandmother has connections all over this town. What in the world were you thinking?"

It takes every ounce of my new restraint not to fling the same question back: What were you thinking when you screwed Kiera and decided to keep the kids? Do you know the damage you caused our family? Instead, I sit silent. I've learned my lesson about speaking up.

Four adults. Forty-five minutes. I was pinned to a desk while they droned on about my unearned privilege and the family name fixing my messes. Apparently, the lecture wasn't enough punishment.

"You have no idea what you've done," Dad snaps, frantic. "We had to leave work. Kiera's stranded with the twins. Even your grandmother had to put herself on the line for you. Do you ever think about anyone but yourself?"

The irony is a physical weight, pressing me deeper into the backseat. My father's priorities are only about maintaining appearances. He isn't mad I defied the law; he's terrified I exposed the loophole protecting him. I look at the back of his head, wondering how many other 'Defenders' are cowards hiding behind a badge and a family name. The DPU light glows a steady, mocking green. For now, the system thinks I'm compliant. It has no idea I'm just getting started.

Mom sits quietly in the passenger seat, but her eyes meet mine in the rearview mirror. They never leave. I wish I could read her mind. She doesn't seem angry. She doesn't even seem disappointed, but without communication, her gaze is unsettling, a constant pressure.

The interior of the car feels smaller now, the air thick with the scent of Gran's expensive perfume and the stale heat of my father's anger. I see her hand rest on the armrest, her fingers still and steady. She isn't breathing fast like Dad. She isn't trembling like me. She is the predator waiting for the right moment to strike. Gran doesn't look at me with anger. Anger is a messy, inefficient emotion—the kind my father uses when he's scared. Instead, she looks at me like a curator looking at a mislabeled exhibit. She doesn't want to punish the outburst; she wants to erase the fact that it ever happened.

"Lincoln, I think she understands her mistake and knows how gracious the consequences are considering," Gran redirects the conversation from beside me, her voice cutting through Dad's rage. "It's about establishing order, not escalating chaos. Don't you Alexandria?"

I don't answer immediately. Gran turns to look at me, her eyes are penetrating, drilling into my silence. She has always been dominant and confident, but her dominance was usually concealed by her niceties. Now I feel a genuine fear of her, a cold certainty she is the real power here. She values control over everything, even her son's rage.

I respond simply and dutifully: "Yes, I understand. Thank you Gran for speaking on my behalf."

I may not know what Gran did behind closed doors, but I saw her work Mr. Everett. When we were all settled, Mr. Everett began to explain the consequences. Gran quickly seized control. "Oh yes, Principal Sterling and I spoke," she asserted, cutting him off. "I assured him Alexandria is not an unstable element. Since this was a first-time offense, authorities wouldn't need to be contacted. We could handle this as a team in-house."

Mr. Everett's irritation was smoothed over by Gran's calm authority. He simply nodded. "Yes, up until this point, there have never been any complaints about Alexandria, so we decided it would be best if her consequences bore a little grace."

I sat there, a bystander to my own fate. Dad and Mom also sat silent, spectators to the private negotiation between Mr. Everett and Gran. "Yes, the solution sounds reasonable," Gran concluded, making it seem like she was merely affirming Mr. Everett's brilliant idea.

Gran uses her signature reassuring-yet-commanding tone with me now. "Of course, Alexandria. We will have plenty of time to discuss this further once everyone has had time to cool down." Her gaze bores into the back of my dad's head. He falls silent, instantly. He knows she is staring directly at him.

The rest of the car ride is silent, broken only by the engine's hum, but Mom's eyes remain locked on mine in the mirror. She doesn't divert even when we make eye contact. I've never felt this noticed and so vulnerable, and it's profoundly unsettling. The tension in her jawline is visible; her fists tightly clench the seat belt buckle, a silent, controlled act of tension.

The decided punishment is meeting with Mr. Everett daily after cross-country practice for an independent study focused on the history and necessity of the Twenty-Ninth Amendment. An hour each day until the end of the semester, with a re-evaluation in mid-January.

I know I am lucky. It could have been so much worse had Principal Sterling decided to report me. I still get to run, and despite my changing perspective, I still love history. In some ways, this is a twisted run.

But my moral compass is spinning widely. This is the very privilege I condemned in my presentation. Because of my family's connections and the positions they hold, I walk away with minimal damage: a mandatory, private re-education. Had it been someone else, their life would be ruined.

We pull up to Gran's house. She gathers her purse, her fingers clinching the clasp. " I'm so glad we'll be having family dinner again. I need you close, Alexandria. Your stability can't be left to chance." She slams the door shut, retreating with a smirk plastered on her face.

Dad waits until he sees Gran safely inside before he pulls the car forward.

"And don't think I haven't thought about the fact your study sessions mean you won't be home to help your mother with dinner," he snaps, regaining his footing now that Gran is gone. "Even the consequences of your actions are impacting the family. Don't worry, I will think of a way for you to earn your keep around the house."

Mom's relentless gaze never abandons me. She is still watching, still taking a silent census of the chaos. I want to go back to being invisible.

# Chapter 16

The rest of the week blurs into a cold, rigid loop.

I wake up at 5:15, an hour earlier than normal. This is Dad's petty revenge. Since I can't be home to prepare dinner before he arrives, I must front-load all the food prep. All Mom has to do when she gets home is slide it into the oven or spend fifteen minutes on the stovetop. Cutting the prep time in half means I'm a servant for longer.

The only upside? Cooking in the mornings is quiet. Charlotte and Savannah are still asleep, and so are Kiera and Dad. Mom shuffles in during the last ten minutes to make the twins' lunches. Most of the time, I work in silence.

Working alone in the stillness, I feel my love of cooking returning. It's no longer about Mom's approval; it's the solace of the process. Chopping vegetables, whisking a marinade—it soothes me, a quiet joy found in creating something beautiful and tangible. It's the highlight of my day, a pleasure I keep tightly to myself since it's meant to be a punishment.

The satisfaction, however, makes for a long day. After cleaning up and packing my backpack, I drag myself to school, begrudging every class.

Senioritis, bitterness—whatever it is, the desire to learn is gone.

I even zone out in History, terrified another outburst might ruin me. I keep my eyes fixed on the grain of the wooden desk, my mouth a sealed vault. I am clutching the shredded hope of a military career— my only escape from Lynn. I keep my hand hovered over the DPU, checking the status light like a pulse. I can't risk another mark. Since my speech stayed off the official report, the military is still an option—the only exit strategy I have left.

I move through the halls with my head down, ignoring the occasional eyes I feel on me. I'm even counting down to the end of cross-country season. Less than two weeks. Right now, nothing holds any purpose except my impending escape.

After practice, I head to Mr. Everett's room, obedient and dutiful. We discuss the value of the Twenty-Ninth Amendment. I recite the official narrative to appease him, but I no longer believe it. What kind of legal system shuts down people for simply asking questions? The rebellious spark from last week is gone. I know my questions will remain unanswered, and the same hypocritical government will unknowingly provide me refuge in a few months. Everything really is give and take.

After a 5:15 start, seven hours of school, a five-mile run, and an hour of Mr. Everett's propaganda, I head home. My body gets a physical rest, but my mind doesn't. I sit at the dinner table with my dysfunctional family. I zone out until I hear my name, which never happens. Dad has tacked on a list of evening chores: wash dishes, help the twins with homework, give them baths. I finish by 11:00 PM, only to wake up and repeat the cycle.

After three days of this monotony, I wake up on Friday with genuine contentment, despite the early morning. I'll have a break after today—no early alarm, no classes, and no Mr. Everett.

Last night, Dad reminded me we are going to Gran's tonight for dinner. He paused—intentionally, I'm sure—before instructing me: "Not to worry, you'll still be preparing dinner. Make sure it feeds everyone, including Gran and Gramps, and is easily transportable."

I chop the cauliflower, sweet potatoes, and Brussels sprouts, coating them in olive oil, paprika, and garlic powder. They will hold until tonight, ready to be roasted on a sheet pan. I hate Brussels sprouts, and I know Charlotte and Savannah will complain, but they're one of Dad's favorites, reminding him of Gramps's comfort food. Learning to prioritize his nostalgia over our own preferences was an early survival requirement.

To even out the selection, I coat pork chops in a barbecue sauce marinade, six-year-old friendly, and drop them into the slow cooker. I don't know why I put this much thought into accommodating everyone. If I made what I wanted, maybe they would stop expecting me to cook.

But it's not the twins' fault. My time with them is limited, and their lives are destined for a level of complication. I want them to remember I cared for them.

As I finish, Mom comes down, "Will you be coming home between school and family dinner?"

"No, I have practice and my study time with Mr. Everett. I'll meet you at Gran and Gramps's house. The vegetables are in the refrigerator. You'll need to bring those to roast there and the slow cooker."

There's no thank you, just a slight acknowledgement and a statement phrased as a question to maintain the veneer of courtesy: "You'll be there on time though?"

"Yes, I will be there by 5:30."

It is the full extent of our communication.

The day drags. Instead of paying attention, I start counting down the days until graduation. I map a countdown in my notebook, tracing the months until I'm free. I track the end of cross-country, and more importantly, the end of my sentence with Mr. Everett.

By History class, my notebook is complete. The projects finished on Wednesday and Mr. Everett is back to lecturing. Cody has permanently claimed my old seat. I'm sitting next to Silas, with his unreadable features and confident swagger. His desire for unrest makes me acutely uneasy. Since our handshake in fifth-grade kickball, his presence affects me. His deliberateness and impassivity are the direct opposite of my recent, impulsive behavior. He sparks controversy with a boldness I envy.

But I'm not Silas. I'm small. I'm inconsequential.

I spend the hour wishing I could be unafraid, but I'm consumed by fear: fear of asking Dad why he cheated, Mom why she's compliant, James why he left, and Gran why our family gets special treatment. I'm plain afraid. After all, I am Alexandria: inconsequential and compliant.

When the bell rings, I get up and Mr. Everett stops me at the door. "Week one is almost complete. See you at 4:00, Alexandria."

Today's practice is in preparation for next Tuesday's meet. I'm still finishing first, but I've been out of tempo all week, not leading anyone. I haven't heard any complaints. Coach Vance probably hopes the shock will wear off, or he knows Mariah will pick up the slack.

"Our last meet was one of our best. We need to finish this season strong. Today and Monday, we'll be practicing two different trails off campus."

Groans rise from the team.

"Today we'll do an eighth of a mile warm-up until we reach the playground on Pennybrook Road. Then we run the Steel Tower, Stone Tower, and Dungeon Rock Loop. It's four and two-tenths of a mile," he explains. "We'll reconvene at the playground and jog back here to cool down."

Shit. The extra mile and a half will significantly extend practice. I can't be late for Mr. Everett, and I absolutely cannot be late for Gran's dinner. If one thing runs late, so does the next, and they all bleed into each other.

Everyone stacks hands, Mariah leads the cheer, and the team yells "Rams!" I don't jog during the warm-up. I bolt toward Lynn Woods, focusing on speed.

I check my watch, the seconds ticking down with cruelty. My lungs are already tight, not from the exertion, but from the fear of the 5:30 deadline. My pace must exceed the limits of the schedule Gran and Dad have built. Perfection is a requirement, or the whole day unravels.

I'm panting when I reach the edge of the woods, where the pavement of the city pushes up against the playground fence. The air here is different —thick with pine and damp earth, a welcome change from the sterile air of the track.

But even this refuge can't escape the system.

Beyond the baseball diamond, facing the main road, sits the Lynn Foster & Allocation Center. It isn't a fancy, modern building; it's a solid, heavy brick structure from another era, repurposed. The grounds are meticulously fenced, and a discreet sign reads: 'Caring for Tomorrow's Citizens.' No one is ever outside, and the curtains are always drawn. It is a silent, permanent reminder of the ultimate consequence of failing the Twenty-Ninth Amendment's Benchmarks—It represents the state's authority to reallocate the children of the non-compliant.

I shove the image out of my mind and turn to the playground. The realization I must wait settles in.

Mariah rounds the corner, her breathing rhythmic and easy, a sharp contrast to the frantic tallying of minutes inside my head.

She looks at me, "You have to study with Mr. Everett after practice, don't you?"

I nod, still catching my breath. So people are still talking.

"If you run with me, I can help set a better pace while leading the others," she suggests. "It'll help us get out of here quicker rather than you trying to bolt on your own. It slows us all down."

I stare at her. "I don't deserve your help after last week. Why are you being so nice to me?"

"It's like I said before, we all have stuff. Why would I want your life to get worse?" Her logic is calm, rational. I can see why Silas likes her. She's driven by logic, a skill I've abandoned.

"Thanks." It's all I can muster. Mariah answers with an authentic smile.

Once everyone is in, Mariah leads the huddle. "Alex and I will lead together running side by side. Watch for our changes in velocity. We'll use Dungeon Rock and Stone Tower as our markers. After Stone Tower, we'll keep our pace until we pass the fork leading to Walden Pond. Then, maximum effort until we finish." Her leadership is natural and efficient. I realize I'm still not a team player, and the military hope wavers again.

"Alright, let's do this!" Mariah taps my arm. We start the run side-by-side.

We take the first mile at seventy-five percent. At Dungeon Rock, we increase to eighty-five percent, Mariah signaling the rest of the team. Running next to her feels strange, but not bad. We are running a little slower than I would alone, but I know we will finish quicker as a unit.

A little over a mile later, we come upon the fork. I turn to Mariah; she gestures back. We surge, pushing to maximum speed for the final mile. It takes five minutes, and Coach is waiting, beaming.

"There it is! I knew you could do it. See what a change of scenery can do? This is exactly how we're going to do it on Tuesday. Alex and Mariah, I expect you to run together. Let's head back to school."

Coach is beaming, but I can't feel the victory. All I can feel is the sweat cooling on my skin and the heavy weight of the history books waiting in Mr. Everett's office. I managed the run, but the day isn't over.

# Chapter 17

Somehow we make it back to campus with barely five minutes to spare. There's no time to shower. The sweat is cold on my skin beneath my damp hoodie. I yank my bag from my locker and head for the door.

Passing Mariah, a sudden impulse makes me stop. "Good run," I manage to say. She smiles, genuine and quick: "Thanks."

I'm not thrilled my last in-season meet as a senior will likely be my slowest personal time, but the run felt different today. I'm content with sacrificing my time for the collective pace.

I walk into Mr. Everett's classroom at exactly 4:00 and stop dead. Silas is sitting at the group of desks where my study materials are laid out.

"What is he doing here?" I blurt out.

"I'm sorry to make your day worse. It already looks like it's been quite rough." Silas's smug voice gives me a once-over. I catch my reflection in the window as the light dims outside. My hair is plastered to my neck and forehead with sweat and dirt. I can feel the damp fabric sticking to my skin. I must reek.

"Sorry, we went off campus for cross-country today and I didn't want to be late," I say to Mr. Everett, ignoring Silas.

"Well I'm glad you're here, but our time is limited," Mr. Everett gestures. "Mr. Wright will be joining us from now on. As promised, I haven't forgotten about his little stunts, and I feel it's fair he receives similar consequences."

A surge of indignation runs through me. Silas, who questioned authority multiple times, is in the same category as me, who made a single, unintentional mistake. But I clamp my mouth shut. I won't point out the hypocrisy.

We begin researching the correlation between the Twenty-Ninth Amendment and financial security. The data is undeniable: after the Amendment passed, people experienced more financial security. Those without procreation approval could still save money by sharing housing, and those who did have children tended to be fiscally responsible. The government saved money on welfare. It's a reminder of the good, and the research is academically intriguing, but I am still counting down the minutes until I can leave. Fifteen more minutes, then the family dinner, then maybe, just maybe, some reprieve.

"I see the correlation, and I know for the vast majority, this is true," Silas says, his voice subdued, a tone of resignation rather than defiance. "But my parents are not part of the mainstream. They're intelligent people, together for a long time, but they have more kids than they can afford."

He explains he, his older brother, and sister were born within five years. They might have been fine, but then his mother unexpectedly became pregnant with twins in ninth grade. I knew Silas had older siblings, but twins?

"My sister was forced to drop out of college after her first year. They couldn't afford to send my brother to college. Now we're all under one roof. It takes my dad, my brother, and my sister working to afford the bills. Mom quit her job to avoid childcare costs for the twins."

Charlotte and Savannah are my half-siblings, yet I feel a crushing responsibility for them. I can't imagine the weight on Silas and his older siblings.

I look at the side of his head, at the curtain of dark hair hiding his expression. In ninth grade, I thought he was being difficult. Now I realize he was mourning. While my family was busy hiding our twins to save our reputation, his family was likely drowning in the cost of theirs. No wonder he looks at the school—and me—with such quiet vitriol.

"They still have two years until they can go to school full-time. I'm not sure how we'll make it without my brother and sister's salaries, but they're going to be ready to move out soon."

Silas's face softens. I see the raw worry and the burden he carries. This is the 'family stuff' Mariah hinted at. Our situations are different, but neither is easy, especially when we're constantly told how lucky we are.

Silas and I make eye contact. The shared knowledge is sharp, a silent acknowledgement of our common burden. It makes me intensely uncomfortable. I break the gaze, snapping my eyes to the clock on the wall.

"Oh shit. I've stayed too long," I gasp, scrambling up. It's 5:25. Outside, the window is a deepening slate gray of dusk. I'm dirty, sweaty, and there's no way I'll make it by 5:30.

I have no choice but to run the straightest, quickest route toward Gran's. It cuts right past my house. Even without the prior six miles and the exhaustion of my week, the 1.6 miles would take me eight minutes. I go full speed. The accumulation of all the 5:15 AM wake-ups, the cooking, the school, the running, and the studying crushes me. The first mile, which should take me five minutes, takes nearly six and a half.

It's 5:37 PM. Dad is going to be livid. I sprint past my house; the driveway is empty, the windows dark. They are waiting for me.

I walk into Gran's at 5:41 PM, breathless and disheveled. The living room is empty, no Gramps snoring. The sound of quiet murmurs and the clinking of silverware draws me to the kitchen. Charlotte and Savannah are unnaturally quiet.

I put my backpack down, take a huge, shuddering breath, and walk into the room, launching immediately into my defense.

"I'm sorry I'm late, but—"

"Yay! Alex is here!" Charlotte and Savannah chirp in unison. I ignore them, focused on Dad's face, now seconds from detonating.

Gran, checking her watch, says: "Punctuality is the cornerstone of discipline, Alexandria."

"Practice was off campus—it went later than normal. Then my session with Mr. Everett ran late, too. I ran the whole way. I'm sorry, I really am."

Mom looks at me, a brief, sympathetic flicker in her eyes—a look I haven't seen in years. It's a tiny relief.

"How are the pork chops?" I ask the twins.

Savannah rushes to answer, "They're my—"

Dad cuts her off, his voice low and dangerous "You're the reason behind all this, and you dare to show up late and then act like everything is normal?"

The sympathy vanishes from Mom's face. I should have known her look was a warning.

"I'm sorry I'm late, Dad, but there's nothing I could do. I got here as quickly as I could."

"There are no excuses," he snarls. "Family comes first, and your actions this week make it blatantly clear you don't care about this family."

I'm frozen. If I get food, he'll see it as a disregard. If I speak back, it's disrespectful. I'm trapped.

"Alexandria, finish filling your plate and sit down," Gran says, her voice not consoling, but a cold, measured attempt to subdue the hysteria. I'm thankful for her intercession.

I place vegetables on my plate, carefully minimizing the hated Brussels sprouts. Mom's back is rigid and her silence is heavy, but she's watching the room. Dad's eyes are burning into me.

"No, Mom," he says indignantly, "You've protected her enough. It's time she starts pulling her weight around here. If Alexandria thinks she's grown up enough to say and do as she pleases, she will start having adult responsibilities."

He makes it sound like I do nothing.

"Then, when she's graduated and has her diploma, she can move out on her own since she has no respect for this family and all we've done for her."

I'm in disbelief. Dad has never stood up to Gran, the matriarch. And why is this coming now? Until Monday, he barely spoke to me.

Everyone is quiet. Gramps, Kiera, and the twins stare at their plates. Gran is expressionless, calculating her next move. I realize now how calculated she is. Dad is the opposite—calm and collected until he explodes.

Dad mutters a final word under his breath as he turns to eat the food I prepared: "Ungrateful."

The air in the room suddenly feels too thin to breathe. I don't see Dad anymore; I see the hypocrisy of every morning spent over a stove, every mile run in silence, and every lie I've told to keep his world from cracking. He wants to talk about family? Fine. Let's talk about what he's done to ours.

"Me ungrateful?" I hear myself yell. "As you sit there and eat the food Mom and I prepared for you, and not one utterance of thanks, not in all these years!"

I grab my plate and dump my vegetables onto his, "Everything centers around your whims—from these disgusting Brussels sprouts to the exact second we sit down."

I slam the empty plate down. It hits the counter. The sound of the ceramic cracking against the granite is the loudest thing in the room—louder than my yelling, louder than the twins' gasping.

Savannah's eyes are wide. Tears form in Charlotte's. I don't care. I've been putting everyone else first for too long.

"You call me selfish. The irony is astounding. What were you thinking when you screwed Kiera and then decided to keep the kids? Do you know what it did to our family?" I drag out the word 'our,' hoping it cuts both Dad and Kiera.

I'm on a roll now, the truth a furious river. "You think I'm not adult enough yet I do more around the house than your childish mistress who doesn't even work. Don't worry, I'll spare you the next seven and a half months, I'll move out now. Good luck finding someone to do all your bidding."

I storm out of the kitchen. I dare not look back. If I see Charlotte, Savannah or even Mom, I may take pity and surrender. I grab my bag from the living room, slam the door behind me, and start running.

I have nowhere to go. My only quasi-friends are Mariah and Silas. Gran has always been my safe haven, and she is now part of the enemy. I'm on a ticking clock to get inside and get back outside.

I run the four blocks, unlock the front door, and bolt upstairs.

Emptying my backpack, I replace it with the essentials: laptop, earbuds, phone, chargers, toiletries, school notebooks, my journal, and the memory box. The duffel bag gets stuffed with layers: underwear, bras, socks, pants, a hoodie, a coat, and a dress. I put on long johns, shorts, sweats, two shirts, and my winter coat. I am overstuffed and rigid, my movements hindered by the bulk. Already I'm starting to sweat, but the weight of the extra shirts feels like ballistic armor. I might not be able to run, but I don't even know where I'm going.

I pause at the threshold of my room, a wave of sadness washing over the anger. I'm glad to be done with this place, but I grieve the normal life I wish I'd had.

I turn back to my desk, grab a pen and paper, and write two identical notes for the twins: "None of this is your fault. I love you always, Alex."

I slip a note under each of their pillows so Kiera won't see them

When James and I were kids we used to sneak into Mom and Dad's room. James once found a pill bottle in their medicine cabinet full of money. So, I head straight for their bathroom. The medicine cabinet is packed with containers. I quickly push past the standard meds, bandages, and the box of condoms—thank God no one else is being brought into this house—and focus on the prescriptions. I spot a bottle of Lexapro prescribed to Mom and another for Dad, Ceftriaxone. I snap a quick picture of both to look up later.

Then I see it: a Plan B box. Jackpot. Not only money, but proof of secrecy. I take a handful of tens and twenties, and stuff it deep into my coat pocket.

I walk out of the bathroom, down the steps, and through the front door, stepping onto the street where I have lived for eighteen years, hoping, praying, it's for the last time. The air is biting, but for the first time in a week, I can breathe.

# Chapter 18

It's 8:00 PM, and I'm slumped on the cold, hard school track, weighing my options. I'm utterly exhausted. The bleachers might block the wind through the night, but it's late October, and the temperature is quickly dropping toward freezing. It's a bad idea, but I have no other immediate solution.

My mind keeps going back to James. I've never been to his place, but I know his address—I snapped a picture of it on Mom's dresser years ago. Calling him feels awkward. Our birthday calls are always five minutes of surface-level conversation about school and cross-country. This version of James feels like a stranger. Yet, he is the only person I can picture going to at this moment.

I know if I call, he'll be the sensible one, urging me to apologize to Dad and go home until graduation. He's always been deliberate, like Gran. His diligent work as a teenager was an exit strategy we didn't even know he was planning.

It's my only plan. Silas and Mariah are non-options; I don't have their contact info and Silas's family is already financially strained.

My phone battery is hovering at twenty-two percent. The Blue Line leaves the terminal at 8:30 and 9:20. If I hurry, I can make the 9:20.

Running is out of the question; the bags and my frantic layers weigh me down. I must walk, going slower than my internal panic allows. Music is a luxury I've forfeited; I'm rationing my battery until I find James.

Walking through the Lynn Common, I try to picture James's life. He works at the Sterilization Center, helping the state decide who gets to have a family and who doesn't. I wonder if he sees the irony in our family's mess. He lives within walking distance of his office. Boston is thirty minutes away, yet I barely know it. The rare city visits were for school field trips or mandatory family outings.

Turning the corner, the wind whips my hair across my face, and I pass the Lynn Wellness Clinic. The building is all bright glass and sterile white siding, with a sign reading, 'Dedicated to the Health of Our Community.' I pick up my pace. It has always felt too quiet, too clean, a constant, polite reminder of where the system sends those it deems unworthy, all disguised behind a veneer of 'wellness.'

The final two miles to the terminal drag on, a slow, physical punishment. I've been going non-stop since 5:15—chores, school, running, studying, screaming, and fleeing. I'm physically and emotionally bankrupt.

I arrive at the terminal at  9:15. By the time I have my ticket and make it onto the bus there are two minutes to spare. Coated in grime and sweat, I'm a walking stink bomb of exhaustion and adrenaline. My disheveled hair, the bags, and the stench are my invisible shield, keeping the few other passengers away and an empty seat beside me.

I doze off, waking to the city lights and the screech of the bus brakes as we enter the downtown streets. We stop at every red light. I check my phone: 9:55 PM. A missed call notification flashes: Mom. She never calls.

I stare at her name, tempted to call back the line connecting me to my old life, but I clear the notification and shove the phone back in my pocket. A few more minutes.

Exiting the bus, a surge of adrenaline hits me. I can't believe I told my dad off in front of everyone. It's both exhilarating and terrifying.

I pull up my map, the screen fading with nineteen percent battery, and head toward James's building.The buzzer is the final hurdle. I press it. Silence. I try twice more. Nothing.

Friday night. It slams into me. James and Brooklyn could be out, or away for the weekend. I am here, in a strange city, past 10:00 PM, with no plan. I slump down in exhaustion and resignation, leaning against the cold brick. I have no choice but to wait.

The streets are busier than I expected. Groups of people stroll by, their laughter and chatter ringing in the bitter air. When they pass me, most look away. But I catch pitying looks, and then the cutting remarks.

"I thought the Twenty-Ninth Amendment was supposed to get rid of the dregs of society."

The realization hits me hard: with my layers, my bags, and my exhausted appearance, I look homeless. The concept only exists in history books and documentaries Gran showed me. She'd point out photos of beachfront encampments from the days before the Amendment, saying, "I'm so thankful for the Twenty-Ninth Amendment. Because of it, you and I never faced a choice like theirs."

I look down at my bulky, distorted shadow on the pavement. I'm a ghost from a history lesson. Gran thought the Amendment saved us from the streets, but she never mentioned that the streets are exactly where you end up when you refuse to play the game.

Did I make the right decision walking away tonight?

I try to rest against the brick, using my duffel as a pillow for my back, and hug my knees to my chest.

The laughter of men a few feet away startles me awake. Walking toward me, I hear a familiar voice.

"Alex, is that you?"

It's hard to make out his face through the harsh glare of the streetlights, but I know it's him.

"Hey James, it's me," I stutter, still disoriented.

"I'm sorry Jeremy. I have to cut the night short. Catch you soon," James says to his friend, then walks toward me, offering a hand. I take it, and only as his strength pulls me up do I realize how weak and cold I am.

"Where's Brooklyn?" I ask, my question as an attempt at normalcy.

"She's out with friends. She should be home soon." He slings my backpack over his left shoulder, grabs the duffel, and gently places his right hand on my shoulder blade. "Let's go in and get warm."

I follow him up one flight of stairs. He enters the apartment with a key code. It's bigger than I expected for the city. James deposits my bags by the door and motions to the couch. "Why don't you sit down? I can make you something to eat." So much about his mannerisms and reactions mirror Gran, providing me with a much needed relief.

"I'd appreciate it. I haven't eaten since lunch, but can I use your bathroom first?"

"Of course. It's in the hallway, the second door on the right."

It's bizarre. We lived together for eleven years, but I don't know the layout of his life. We are strangers now.

The walls are modern and warm, with artwork but no photographs. The first door is closed, but the bathroom door is slightly ajar.

Washing my hands, I catch a glimpse of myself in the mirror. I look even more haggard than I imagined. The linen closet is neatly stocked with towels, medicines, toiletries, and–condoms. It's a jarring reminder that my brother is a twenty-five-year-old man, sharing an adult life I know nothing about, a life built on responsible choice, unlike the secrets I left behind.

The soap is unscented and clinical, cutting through the salt of my sweat. Watching the grey water swirl down the drain, I feel a fraction of the week's weight lift. I dry off, pull my t-shirt and hoodie back on, and find a comb to tame my hair. I'm still cold, but I feel and smell marginally better.

Walking back out, I see two other closed doors further down the hall. A three-bedroom apartment in the city is a fortune in credits. James isn't just surviving; he has achieved a level of stability I can't even fathom.

James has a mug of tea waiting for me on the coffee table. He's stirring something on the stove. "I'm not sure you like tea, but I figured it would warm you up."

"I do. Thanks." We are now strangers who don't know each other's drink preferences. I've longed for my brother, but I'm suddenly unsure if I missed him or the idea of him.

He walks over with two bowls. "It's a pre-made butternut squash soup. I'm no chef like you, but I hope you like it," he says, sitting in the armchair across from me.

The smell of soup hits me, and suddenly I'm ravenous. I cup my hands around the bowl. I burn the roof of my mouth, but the heat flows down my throat and thaws my chest. I've never enjoyed pre-made soup so much.

James is handling this with an easy, quiet calm. He didn't react with panic or questions; he went straight to making food. He casually referenced my cooking. He sat down to eat with me, not just serve me. All of it makes me feel more at home than I have in ages. He is the order I always wanted, free of ingrained compliance.

We sit in silence for a few minutes, the only sounds the clink of spoons and sips of tea. I appreciate his kindness, but I'm anxious for the inevitable questions. I savor the soup, committing to memory the way it's thawing me from the inside out. I'm starting to feel like myself again.

I look at the kitchen clock. It's after midnight. "I'm sorry it's so late. I don't want to bother—"

"Let me stop you right there. You're not bothering me." James interrupts gently. "We can catch up in the morning. You can stay in the guest room," he points to the first closed door. "Brooklyn should be home soon. I'll let her know you're here."

I want to hug him, tell him everything, but I barely manage, "Thanks, James."

# Chapter 19

The sound of low, indiscernible voices beyond the guest room pulls me from a deep, almost catatonic sleep. Sunlight blasts through the window. I feel like I've slept for three days. I grab my phone off the charger. Another missed call from Mom early this morning. I clear the notification. It's almost 10:00 AM. Yesterday was one of the longest days of my life, rivaled only by the night our family broke apart when I was eleven. Both felt cataclysmic.

With the phone charged, I dive into searching. Lexapro. It treats anxiety and major depressive disorders. Mom is depressed? I plunge down a rabbit hole, checking side effects and symptoms. I hate my own ignorance—I never knew she was struggling. Her shifting moods and distant communication were likely symptoms of an illness. It's genetic. Does it explain my difficulty forming friendships or trusting people?

Ceftriaxone. An antibiotic used for sexually transmitted infections, like gonorrhea.

Between the Ceftriaxone and the Plan B, my last shreds of guilt about stealing cash and running away evaporate. Dad is still screwing around. Whether Kiera is his sole focus or merely one of many, the reality remains revolting—not just the image, but the blatant, sustained hypocrisy. He does whatever he wants, and everyone looks the other way.

Rage coils in my stomach. I slam the phone onto the nightstand, closing my eyes and taking a deep breath.

I catch a faint, sweet smell of pancake batter, quickly overpowered by the sharp, pungent smell of bacon. My stomach rumbles. The batter smells like Gran's recipe.

My nerves are clawing at me. I can't lie here anymore. I take a quick, steamy shower, washing off the same grime as yesterday. Clean sweatpants, a T-shirt, and a zip-up hoodie. I open the door and walk silently into the hallway.

Brooklyn and James have their backs to me, deep in conversation. She's at the stove; he's whisking batter. I notice the animated movement of Brooklyn's tongs. I take a few steps back into the doorframe to listen.

Now that we've all rested, the reality of my arrival must settle in. James was kind last night—no prying, no questions—but I can't imagine Brooklyn is thrilled to have a runaway teenager in her home. My parents had no choice but to house me; James and Brooklyn owe me nothing.

I strain to make out the words.

"You need to tell her," Brooklyn says, tongs raised. I can't catch James's response. My stomach tightens. They're making breakfast to soften the blow. They're going to tell me I can't stay.

Brooklyn moves the bacon to a plate. James hands her the bowl of batter, and she pours it onto the hot griddle. It's oddly fascinating to watch them work —the intimacy, the non-verbal cues. I never saw Mom and Dad cook together. It was always Mom and me.

Brooklyn flips a pancake. James turns to grab three plates from the cabinet and stops, his eyes finding mine.

"Good morning, Alex. Come join us."

Brooklyn immediately turns, handing James the spatula, and walks toward me. "Hey Alex," she says, pulling me into a hug. The casual, friendly gesture feels both alien and wonderful.

"Yeah, thanks for letting me crash here. Sorry, I didn't get to see you."

"No, I'm sorry. If I knew you were coming, I would have made sure I was home. But we're all here now." She waves me forward. "Come, we're making breakfast. It's almost done."

I follow her to the table. Sleeping in, having someone cook for me, and being spoken to without expectation is a rare luxury. Instead of soothing me, it puts me on edge. I question the intent behind every kindness.

Within minutes, three plates—bacon and pancakes—are placed on the table, along with a hot cup of tea. For a moment, I miss Mom, our cooking ritual, and Gran's comfort food.

Brooklyn and James sit down and start eating. I follow their lead, forcing myself to slow my frantic chewing. We don't eat like this at home, where meals are health-conscious, heavy on vegetables, and light on carbs—Dad's preferences, dictated by Gran.

I break the silence. "We never eat like this at home." It sounds ridiculous the moment it leaves my mouth.

"It's one of the best parts about being an adult and having your own place. You get to decide what you eat," Brooklyn says, looking between James and me. James is quieter this morning, letting Brooklyn lead.

She clears her throat, then asks directly, "So how is home?"

I immediately regret bringing it up.

"Brooklyn." James warns her with a look. Then, to me, "We really don't have to jump right into it, Alex."

"He's right. We're glad you're here," Brooklyn confirms.

I can't stand the niceties. "No, it's okay. I showed up unannounced. It's only fair you get to ask questions."

"Home has been hard," I start. "It's been hard for as long as I can remember. Things weren't great before you left, and they've gotten worse." Sadness overcomes James's face. I hurry to recover. "I don't blame you though. You had a chance to get away from the chaos. I've realized recently I would do the same." I think of Charlotte and Savannah.

Brooklyn gives James a deliberate, nudging look. I can already see their subtle, intimate language.

"It's part of it, Alex, but it's not all of it," James says, sighing. "I want to tell you I'm sorry for leaving you there alone. I was young, and I felt I didn't have a lot of choice."

I stay quiet. It felt like a deliberate choice then, but I know contradicting him won't help.

He nods, urging himself on. "I would have taken you with me if I could have, but you were a minor. I was only eighteen myself. I couldn't legally adopt you. I knew the law wouldn't allow it."

He's stating pure logic, but I never considered it. A wave of guilt for my years of bitter assumption washes over me.

"I've been working hard these last seven years," he continues, looking tenderly at Brooklyn, "moving up in my job, buying an apartment. I wanted to make sure by the time you graduated high school, I had an environment capable of including you—if you wanted it."

All this time, James was planning a future for me, and I thought he'd forgotten I existed.

"Why didn't you ever say anything?"

"I didn't want Dad or Mom to stop it. I thought if they knew, they'd find a way to make sure you couldn't come stay with me—lie, or even use the government to declare me unfit. We were waiting until you turned eighteen and graduated. Then it would be your choice as an adult."

After years of feeling invisible, unwanted, and abandoned, I struggle to accept this sincerity. "I thought you forgot about me. I was seriously considering the military, but after the last week, I'm not sure I believe in it anymore."

The silence following my words feels heavy. In James's world, the military and the Centers are the pillars of a functioning society. I wait for the 'sensible' brother to argue, but instead, I see the flicker of sadness in his eyes.

"What do you mean, you don't believe in anymore?" James asks.

My natural inclination is to shut down, run, and process alone. But James and Brooklyn wait— silent and attentive. I'm not used to being asked questions, or sharing my inner thoughts.

Gran's voice echoes in my head, a warm, soft lullaby about the 'bad old days.' I used to find comfort in her certainty. Now, that certainty feels like a wall she built to keep me from looking too closely at the cracks in our foundation. I'm looking now, and I can't stop.

"We were taught all our lives how lucky we are for the Twenty-Ninth Amendment," I hesitantly begin. "In school, we repeat it. Our families preach it. All those Friday nights at Gran's, watching documentaries, hearing the stories." I think of Gran, my one constant. I hate questioning her now. Does someone have to be all good for me to love them, or all bad for me to hate them?

"I understand," Brooklyn reaffirms me. "I went to the same schools. We were constantly told how lucky we were."

"Also, you do know Gran basically approves the curriculum for Massachusetts schools, right? She's the Massachusetts Secretary of Education," James says, rolling his eyes.

I stare at him. "I thought she was retired." The pieces snap together: Gran's love of history, her documentation, her insistence on order.

"She's semi-retired, but powerful enough to be heard."

"And to keep all her contacts," Brooklyn adds.

My brain explodes with connections. Our family's privilege is deeper than I realized. "Did Dad have a choice about Charlotte and Savannah because Gran knew people in the Lynn municipality?" I don't let either one of them answer. I surge forward, "It's why I'm questioning the Twenty-Ninth Amendment.

It may be beneficial in theory, but not everyone is held to the same standard. Allowances are made for people like Dad, and even me, simply because of who our family is. It's not fair."

James looks confused. "I guess I'm still not sure what you're saying you don't believe. Are you saying you disagree with the implementation of the Amendment, or you don't believe life is overall better because of it?"

"I'm starting to think everything is not as black and white as it's made out to be," I echo Gran's words. The passion from Mr. Everett's class flares up. "Think about our situation, James. Dad cheated. We all dealt with the consequences. None of us have the family intended by the Amendment."

"Sure, life wasn't easy, but my memories aren't all bad. You have good memories too—cooking with Mom, time at Gran's," James argues, trying to convince me. His life didn't drastically change until he was nearly an adult. I've dealt with it the last seven years. I realize I'm dependent on them. I can't push too far.

"Even with laws, nothing is perfect. People are still human," he adds.

I try a logical angle. "Regardless of the Amendment, Dad got Kiera pregnant and the Lynn municipality gave him a choice most people wouldn't get. I spoke out at school. Gran got involved with the principal to prevent a government report. Corruption still exists; it's only quieter."

"Wait, you spoke out at school?" Brooklyn asks, visibly shaken.

I seize the interruption. The government talk is pushing James.

"That's kind of why I'm here. I asked these same questions during a presentation. My teacher got mad, called Mom and Dad. Gran stepped in, but gave our parents stipulations—like reinstating Friday dinners. Dad had been treating me like a servant. We had a huge blowup at Gran's last night." I pause, the resignation heavy in my voice. "I don't think I can go back there. I'm not sure I can last until graduation. I'm exhausted and running on fumes."

The room falls silent. I know it's a lot to process. I chew a piece of pancake, wanting to crawl under the table. I'm afraid of being a burden; I've felt like one for too long.

I break up the tension. "I mean I'm not asking–"

"We were already planning—"James starts simultaneously.

I let him continue. He's the one with the power here.

"We were already planning on having you stay here with us once you graduated. The room you're in was already set for you."

"We know things haven't been great," Brooklyn adds. "We feel really guilty, but the law didn't really allow us to do this until a few months ago, and we thought we could make it a few more months. But sometimes easy isn't what's best."

"Thank you so much," I say. It feels inadequate. I worry about being an inconvenience, about the logistics—school transfer, guardianship.

"We need to be careful though," James cautions. "I don't want to jeopardize my job, and you don't want to give the administration any more reasons to report you. We need to think through this to avoid serious repercussions."

I ask, without thinking: "Why would you want to keep working somewhere so deceitful and immoral?"

A flash of frustration crosses James's face. "It's not black and white, Alexandria. It's a job, and in my case, it's a good one."

"We understand your outrage," Brooklyn interjects, firm but kind. "But both of our government jobs keep us financially responsible. They provided for us and allowed us to make this space our home and offer it to you. We are not willing to risk them."

They are willing to risk me, but not their livelihood. Their escape from the system's emotional demands is still dependent on the system's financial rewards. The rules still apply, even to the good guys.

"I'm sorry. I really don't want to cause any problems. Maybe I should go back home."

"No, no, no," Brooklyn insists. "We've already decided. This is what's best for you. We need some time to figure out how to handle it."

"Thank you," I repeat. "I don't want to be rude, but do you guys mind if I go for a run before I finish this food?"

"Of course," Brooklyn says immediately.

"This gives us some time to process and come up with a plan while you're out before we run it by you," James adds.

The use of 'we' and the exclusion of me from the planning hurts. It's another reminder James has moved forward. I'm not sure I really belong in this life they've built, even though they're inviting me into it.

"Sounds good." I put my plate on the counter and walk toward my new bedroom to get ready for my run.

# Chapter 20

James and Brooklyn didn't waste the weekend. They filed the initial legal paperwork for both guardianship and adoption. Even though I'm eighteen, they decided a legal foundation was the safest route, protecting their steady, government-affiliated jobs. James recently earned a promotion at the Sterilization Facility, and Brooklyn maintains a stable position, splitting her time between remote data entry and surveys with physical research in the field. This demonstrated stability will be their primary evidence they're capable of taking me in. Their freedom is contingent on their compliance.

Part of the plan requires me to remain in Lynn High School. If I withdraw now, or stop meeting with Mr. Everett, the administration might report me. They also reasoned the school had a vested interest in keeping me quiet; my performance in cross-country, track, and possibly swimming could secure regional titles, boosting the school's status.

Since Brooklyn works from home most days, she's taking the morning commute. We need to leave by 6:15 AM to account for her return traffic to Boston. I woke up surprisingly well-rested despite the stress. I'll have almost an hour at school before class—time I plan to use for homework or maybe a short run. I'm grateful they are making this work.

The drive is quiet. Brooklyn attempts small talk, asking about my classes and friends. I'm not trying to be rude, but I am talked out. I've never shared so much in my entire life as I did this weekend. I give her curt, one-sentence replies. She gently checks for the third time that her and James's numbers are in my phone, and I nod. Taking the hint, she switches on the radio.

As she pulls up to the school curb, I politely offer my gratitude, "Thanks for the ride."

"Of course. Are you okay to take the bus after practice and your meeting with your teacher?"

It's a forty-five minute ride from Lynn to Boston—and I need every second of it. It's a guaranteed period of decompression and solitude after a day of forced interaction.

"Yep, no problem. I'll see you later tonight. Have a good day." Brooklyn's pleasantries are already sticking to me, even if they sound unnatural.

The halls are cleaner and quieter than I've ever seen them. I pass classrooms, some still dark, others open with teachers preparing for the day. There are small study groups clustered in two of the rooms.

Mr. Everett's light is on, but the door is closed. I peer through the small window and see him and Silas sitting at the desks in the back corner, notebooks spread open between them.

Without thinking, I open the door, "No one told me we were meeting in the mornings now."

Both look up, startled. Mr. Everett recovers quickly. "Good morning Alexandria. Mr. Wright has been more of a consistent issue than you, so I thought it was only fair he had some extra time with me. But you are more than welcome to join us."

The atmosphere is surprisingly relaxed. Silas seems at ease.

"I'm sorry I ran out on Friday. I didn't mean to be so rude, but I had some family obligations and—"

"It's okay," Silas cuts in, "I'm sorry I shared so much and made it awkward. You probably didn't want to hear all of that."

He's trying to clear the air, but the truth is I needed to hear it. Internally, my world has been centered on my own suffering—my father ruined my life, my mother is emotionally absent, James abandoned me. Silas's confession was a harsh, necessary reality check.

"Actually, it was nice to hear someone else has family problems for once," I admit. I immediately flinch. "I don't mean that I want you to have problems or anything."

I see a genuine smile break through Silas's usual smirk. His small gesture puts me at ease, and I join them at the desks.

"So now that I've shared way too much about my family, I feel like—" Silas trails off, raising his eyebrows at me.

"I'm pretty sure you've already heard all about my family," I counter, the light mood encouraging me. "Maybe it's time he shares," I nod toward Mr. Everett.

Everyone chuckles. Is this what having friends feels like?

"Well if it helps to know a little about me, I'm happy to share." I'm surprised. Mr. Everett, the fervent history teacher, is showing us the human beneath the tweed jacket.

"I can't say I can relate to a lot of your family struggles," he begins. "My sister and I had a good childhood. We definitely reaped the benefits of the Twenty-Ninth Amendment."

His naive, sheltered tone explains a lot of his classroom rants. His childhood was saturated with patriotism of the generation living through the societal shift.

"It inspired me to become a teacher. I could feel the sense of pride oozing from my grandfather and his friends when they shared how President Wolf had made their lives better.    I felt it was worth preserving."

Despite my current resentment, I relate to his fervor. A few weeks ago, I considered a future as a museum archivist, driven by the same passion for Gran's photo albums.

"To preserve order, we must keep an accurate account of history." The words taste like copper in my mouth. I didn't choose to say them; they were there, waiting in the back of my throat like a reflex.

Silas stares at me, his smirk faltering for a split second. He recognizes the textbook cadence. We both do.

"Well, like you Alexandria, I came to a crossroads in my life where I started questioning— just a bit later in life."

It's startling to hear Mr. Everett, the zealous protector of the Amendment, admit to doubt. His admission doesn't feel like a betrayal; it feels like a hand reaching out in the dark. I'm not the only one pretending.

"My wife and I were married at twenty-three. We were eager to have children. We met all the benchmarks. When I turned twenty-five, I underwent the reverse sterilization process. Something went wrong. When I came out of surgery, they told my wife and me it was unsuccessful. I had a disease preventing me from having children. We were devastated." His voice wavers. "I spent days in the hospital, physically recovering, but they were afraid to send me home. I was so distraught."

My stomach drops. I hadn't considered the personal toll of my presentation last week. The moment I mentioned difficulties conceiving, Mr. Everett snapped. His anger wasn't patriotism; it was unprocessed grief enforced by the system he preaches.

"It felt like I had no purpose," he continues, his gaze distant. "Because of the importance placed on the benchmarks, having children became my ultimate dream. If I couldn't have kids, what was the point of a steady job, saving money, maintaining a successful partnership? It felt like a waste." I relate to the feeling of a pre-determined future being stolen.

"The last night I was there," he says, leaning forward, his voice a low conspiracy, " one of the nurses told me I wasn't actually sick. They were using the diagnosis of a disease as a cover. The doctor had made a mistake during the surgery."

My breath hitches. A mistake. In the world of the Twenty-Ninth Amendment, mistakes don't exist—only "unforeseen variables" or "medical anomalies." To admit a doctor failed is to admit the system is fallible, and the system's entire authority rests on the illusion of perfection.

I look at Mr. Everett, realizing the depth of the gaslighting he's endured. They took his ability to have children; they stole his right to be angry about it by handing him a fake diagnosis. They turned his grief into a "pre-existing condition" so he couldn't blame the state.

Silas breaks the heavy silence, "So do you think they did it on purpose, or is it a common mishap?"

"I don't think it was intentional, but I doubt I'm the first." Mr. Everett shakes his head. "We looked into adoption, but because of population control, there isn't an excess of children like there once was. We felt cheated. We were taught if we met the benchmarks, we'd be able to experience parenthood. We chose to, and it was taken from us."

His pain is an agonizing punch. I've been so self-centered.

"So how did you move past your questioning and keep teaching history where you have to unequivocally back the government?" I ask, genuinely curious for my own sake.

"My wife and I couldn't live near our family anymore; the nieces and nephews were a constant reminder. We moved here from Philadelphia. Three years ago, we decided to take our names off the adoption waitlist. Losing the last shred of hope motivated me in other areas. Since I couldn't instill patriotism in my own kids, I became more zealous and dedicated in the classroom."

"Yes, you did," Silas remarks, and an uninhibited laugh escapes me.

"I know, I know. Truth is, I've been suppressing my doubts, pushing down my frustrations, making excuses. But hearing you two these last few weeks evoked a resentment and indignation I thought I'd diffused."

Hearing Mr. Everett's admission reignites the fury in my chest. "So why let it go? We're three people in one tiny town who have discovered we have negative repercussions associated with the

Twenty-Ninth. We know because we've actually talked about it. But what about everyone else?"

"She's right," Silas affirms. "No one talks because they're scared they'll be reported, but there are more of us. We shouldn't be quiet about it."

"Our ancestors weren't quiet about the change they wanted," I press, looking at Mr. Everett. "Maybe it's served its purpose, and now we need to speak up too."

"We want to make sure we're not being reckless or acting out of emotion." Mr. Everett says, his tone shifting back to a cautious textbook recitation: "With too much information all at once, we're more liable to make brash decisions."

"I know, I've heard it many times before: 'Too much of anything isn't good for anyone.' Well, maybe we've had too much of the Twenty-Ninth Amendment," I challenge. I draw a sharp, jagged breath, my lungs burning as if I've just finished a sprint. I wait for the walls to crumble or the sirens to start. I've committed the one sin Gran's curriculum doesn't forgive: I questioned the necessity of our existence.

"Mr. Everett, you have felt what we have. Maybe together we can make a difference. Think about it." I look from Silas to Mr. Everett, realizing I didn't just share a thought—I declared a war.

The bell rings, the five-minute warning for the start of the day. Mr. Everett stands up and walks to the board to prepare for his class, leaving us hanging. "I'll see you two in class."

Silas and I look at each other, stunned by the abrupt dismissal. Could he really be shutting down the conversation now? Or is he giving himself time to decide if he will join the rebellion? We stand, grab our bags, and walk out of the room side by side.

# Chapter 21

My mind refuses to settle. I go through my classes on autopilot, doing the minimum to remain invisible. The heavy knowledge of Silas, Mr. Everett, and the Twenty-Ninth Amendment presses down on me. For once, I wish away cross-country practice, the very thing usually saving me. The anxiety is a low hum: What would we have discussed? Could we really have formed a group capable of forcing the municipality to listen?

The thought is terrifying and electrifying.

In the hallway, I spot Mariah and force a smile. It catches her off guard; her own smile lags before she recovers.

"Hi Alex." I keep walking and wave. "See you at practice."

I shuffle into History. Mr. Everett doesn't even look up—he utters the standard, emotionless "Alexandria." I slump into my seat next to Silas. We exchange one quick, tense glance: He bottled it up. Mr. Everett launches into his lecture. I zone out, staring at him. How can he switch from confessing governmental betrayal to spitting propaganda? I would be livid. The government took his future. Yet here he is, the loyal parrot.

When the final bell screams, I reach for my bag.

"Mr. Wright, Alexandria, a minute please."

We walk to his desk. "I'm going to have to cancel our meeting until further notice," he states, his voice flat. "The administration will hear nothing of it. Any absence is due to my commitments."

My disappointment is a gut punch. "Wait, that's it? You're giving up?"

Mr. Everett is a wall—impenetrable, composed. "I'll be in touch. Have a good night," he signals toward the door. He wants us out. All my fragile hopes shatter. Another adult chooses security over truth. I hate how he suppresses the same indignation he admitted to twenty-four hours ago.

---

Silas walks out with me. I lean against my locker, the metal cool against my cheek, and let out a heavy sigh.

"Are you okay?" Silas asks. The simple question feels massive.

"A lot happened this weekend," I admit. "I was so hopeful. I thought since Mr. Everett finally resonated with us, we could actually change something."

Silas nods. "I kept pushing because I saw a flash of doubt in him early on. I thought he was different. It means you and I can't stop, but it's going to be harder without him." He talks about "you and I" like we're a team, and my skin flushes hot. I shove the confusing feeling away. Silas is a teammate, an ally— nothing more.

"What happened this weekend?" he presses.

My panic spikes. I can't talk about James and Brooklyn here. "Practice is about to start. Give me your number." We exchange phones, and I feel a desperate need to get away from him before I blurt out everything.

---

I sprint to the field. Practice is a blur of forced strategy: Mariah and I slow our pace to keep the pack together. We run the half mile, hit the trail, and then I turn my focus inward, pushing the team's tempo. My usual escape is hampered by the constant communication.

The strategy works. Everyone but me beats their PRs. As Coach gives his speech, I start walking quickly toward the locker room. Mr. Everett canceled the meeting; I can catch an earlier bus. I want to cook dinner as a thank you to James and Brooklyn.

I'm slamming my locker shut when Mariah jogs up. "Hey, Alex. Mr. Everett canceled? Want to hang out?"

"I have to catch the bus," I say, already moving. "Sorry, I'm in a rush."

Mariah catches my arm. "Wait, take my number. We should plan something before the season ends." Another number saved. I wave goodbye and run toward the terminal.

---

I collapse onto a bus seat. I didn't even have time to put in my earbuds. Someone sits next to me. I glance around; the bus is packed. I pull out my phone to avoid the forced presence of a stranger.

Silas's text waits, "So what happened this weekend?"

As the bus lurches forward, the words stream out of me– the fight, the flight, the decision to stay. Sending the text feels like a release. My phone buzzes instantly: Mariah. "Thanks for sacrificing your PR to help me and the rest of the team. See you tomorrow."

Before today my phone was a desert. Now, I have two text conversations. I spend the entire forty-minute ride engulfed in the exchange with Silas, learning about his older sister and his decision to work to help his family financially despite his scholarships. My thumbs fly across the screen. I shouldn't trust him this much, but he's the only person who knows the Alexandria who fights back.

The ride vanishes.

I slip my phone into my pocket and start planning the salmon pasta.

I climb the stairs to the apartment. Loud, thumping music is blaring. No one should be home. I drop my bag and walk down the hall. Brooklyn's office is empty.

The music is pulsing from James and Brooklyn's bedroom. I bang twice, a sharp, loud rhythm, before yanking the door open.

My vision locks. A blanket is pulled up over my brother and a guy.

"What the hell, Alex?" James's tone is sharp, laced with panic and anger– the sound of the teenage brother who left me behind.

I stare. The familiar face snaps into focus: the same man from Friday night. My confusion boils to sickening rage. Is he cheating? I won't let this happen to Brooklyn.

Anger bubbles up inside me. How could he be unfaithful to Brooklyn after all we went through with Mom and Dad? I will not be silent again. I will not let history repeat itself.

"No, what the hell, James? You're cheating on Brooklyn?"

The man in the bed is frozen, eyes wide with embarrassment. I can't believe I'm still standing here. I spin around, slam the door shut, and yank out my earbuds, blast the music, and bolt out the door for a run.

He is just like my dad. The thought is a relentless, physical pain. Brooklyn is the kindest person I know. I try to zone out, pounding the pavement. My shock starts to wear off, and my emotions coalesce into a cold anger.

I stop at Post Office Square, shivering as the cool evening hits my sweat. It's almost 5:30. I try calling Silas, but there's no answer. I'm desperate. I try calling once more. He cuts off my call but I get a text: "Sorry dealing with some family stuff. Can't talk."

My phone buzzes. Brooklyn. "Hey, James told me what happened. Please come home so we can talk."

Her calm tone is unnerving. My legs ache, my stomach grows. I climb the stairs. Brooklyn is pulling takeout containers onto the table.

"Hey Alex," she puts the food down and opens her arms.

I back away. She needs comforting, not me. Why is she acting so composed?

"What's going on? Why are you acting like this is no big deal, Brooklyn?" I can't stop the words. "He should know better! I'm done being quiet while men walk all over the women I love. You do not deserve this."

A flicker of warmth, of gratitude, crosses her face.

James emerges from the bathroom, hair wet. "I'm sorry you saw that Alex, but it's a little more complicated than it seems. Let me explain."

"There is no explanation. You were cheating! I can't believe you would do this after everything with

Dad. Maybe since you didn't stick around, you don't really know."

James's anger flares. "You're not the only one who's been hurt!. Alex, stop playing the victim and making this all about you."

"At least I'm not like Mom who rolls over, or like you who leaves when things get hard!" His words hurt more than I let on.

James stands firm, but the pain is audible. "Mom was protecting us. I was protecting you. I have spent so much time worrying about you, more than you understand."

"Stop it, both of you!" Brooklyn's voice cuts through the noise, sharp and commanding. "Alex, James is gay. He's been gay as long as I can remember. I've known this about him since high school. Today does not come as a surprise to me. Now, please, let's sit down and talk about it."

The silence following her words is deafening, louder than the thumping music from before. I look at James, then back to Brooklyn. The air in the room shifts. James sinks into a chair. I stare at Brooklyn. Her composure, her directness, the calm authority in her eyes—she and James share a connection so real, it's deeper than anything I ever saw between my parents.

# Chapter 22

Brooklyn sits with us for a few minutes. I study the takeout containers, the scent of soy sauce and ginger strong in the air. I realize their partnership is far more complex than I can grasp right now. Once James and I have both visibly cooled down—our breathing slowing, our shoulders relaxing—Brooklyn stands up.

She grabs her container. "I have a lot of work to do from today's field study. I'm going to go into the office and let you two talk. You know where to find me if you need me."

Brooklyn's ability to read a room is astounding. I've never seen anyone do it the way she does. She knows exactly when to be seen and when not to be. I long for her maturity.

She moves through the world like a shadow—present, yet impossible to pin down. My life has been spent trying to run away from things, but Brooklyn knows how to stand perfectly still and still remain hidden. It's a specialty I haven't mastered yet, and I'll need it to survive the 29th.

I have so many questions, but I worry I've already said too much. James leads the conversation while I focus on the Chinese chicken and broccoli Brooklyn put in front of me.

"I didn't always know I preferred guys," James begins, picking at his rice. "But the more I experimented with girls, the more I knew I didn't really like them. I'd dated a few girls, including Brooklyn. She was by far my favorite person to be around. But whenever we would kiss or do anything more, I wasn't into it. I wasn't sure what it really meant though."

I watch him struggle with the words, the same brother who always has an answer for everything. He wasn't hiding a preference; he was hiding a whole version of himself from a world that values people who fit the mold. The anger that felt like a hot coal in my stomach moments ago begins to cool, replaced by a hollow, aching sort of understanding.

"So how did you figure out you were gay?" I blurt out, momentarily forgetting my resolve to stay quiet.

James pauses, the plastic fork hovering over his container. "In tenth grade, after I'd dated a few girls, I talked to Gran one night. I told her I had a friend who didn't like girls, and I asked her what it meant. She used the word 'homosexual' and explained how some people like the same gender."

He sets the fork down. His eyes are fixed on a spot over my shoulder. "She stayed even-keeled about it, but I could tell from her word choices and tone she didn't approve. Gran was adamant—even if it were legal, it wasn't natural because they couldn't have biological children. She shared a lot about the importance of giving back to society through procreation."

A sadness I've never seen before settles over his face. I realize how little I truly know about him. I saw him as my best friend, but our age difference created a gulf I didn't understand.

"After talking with Gran, it was like a lightbulb went off. I'd never heard the word 'gay' before. I don't remember seeing a same-sex couple in a movie or a book. I spent a few months trying to suppress my curiosities about guys. But once I started working over the summer before junior year, I couldn't help it anymore."

He leans forward, his voice lower. "Coming into the city to work part-time and meeting different, less small-minded people, opened my eyes. I started seeing guys I worked with and others I met around the city."

"I don't understand though," I press. "If you've known this since you lived at home, why pretend you're straight? Why didn't you tell us? You moved out anyway."

James's jaw tightens. "I didn't choose to move out, Alex. Dad gave me an ultimatum."

My stomach clenches. I can't believe Dad forced his own son away. It's not like there is a law against it. Dad is pro-government, and same sex-marriage is legal.

"It must have been really hard to tell Dad," I mutter. "I wish I'd known."

I know how silly it sounds. I was eleven. I wouldn't have understood. Worse, there's a chance I would have gone along with Dad, the way Mom and I always did.

"Honestly, I wish it had been some super serious talk. It wasn't though. You remember I'd leave school at lunchtime junior and senior years to work in the city? I earned work credit, made money, and started building my name at the Sterilization Center, thanks to Gran's connections."

I knew about the part-time job, but I wasn't aware until this weekend of how much power Gran wields.

"All of it was exciting, but really I loved the idea of meeting more people who had differing values than those in Lynn." I imagine sixteen-year-old James navigating Boston—daunting for me, but clearly exhilarating for him.

"I worked every day, but the days off from work didn't always align with my school schedule. Instead of telling anyone, I would take the afternoon off. Sometimes I relaxed at home in the quiet. Other times I'd come into the city and meet friends from work."

He leans closer, his eyes bright with a memory. "The summer before senior year, I met Greg. He worked at the coffee shop nearby. I was the office errand boy, but I went to work every day eager to take everyone's order, so I could see Greg."

Hearing the way he talks about Greg reminds me of Silas. The butterflies I get whenever I think about Silas. I convince myself it's because I haven't had a real friend in so long. Even now, in this intense conversation, I catch myself hoping to hear back from Silas.

James takes my silence as a cue to continue. "We kept seeing each other even after the summer. It was difficult to coordinate. We'd arrange a time to meet once a week when I was in the city. I'm not sure how serious it was in retrospect, but it was my first real relationship. I would wait in anticipation to see him. The afternoons I had off from work senior year became our time."

"Since it was every couple of months, he would skip his classes and ride the bus to Lynn. We always met at the house so no one would see us. We did this a few times, and looking back, it was one of the most thrilling things I've ever done—sneaking around behind Mom and Dad's backs, bringing a boy into the house. I really cared about Greg, but I also loved the secrecy of our relationship."

The revelation about Greg and the sneaking around hangs in the air. James takes a drink of water, and I sense the end of the thrilling part of the story.

"So, what happened to Greg?" I ask.

James shrugs, a quick dismissive motion. "I stopped seeing him. We grew apart, I guess. I realize now how immature I was. I loved the idea of having a boyfriend more than I loved him. But the rush of secrecy is hard to forget."

He leans back in his chair, the lightness gone. "The next semester, Mom and Dad started pushing for me to choose a college. They wanted me to stay local and go to North Shore. I told them I wanted to go to Boston University. I wanted to live in the city, but they shut me down. They dismissed it as a waste of money when a local school was just as good.

James pushes his empty container aside. "That's when I realized the only way I could live my life was to get out of Lynn. I couldn't keep sneaking around. I couldn't keep pretending."

"So you told them?" I breathe.

"No. Not exactly. I tried to get Dad to see my side. I told him I needed to move to the city for opportunities, for the job I had lined up, but he refused to listen. Then, about a month before graduation. I slipped up."

James scrubs a hand over his face, "I was texting one of the guys I met at work. Making plans. Dad walked in and asked who I was talking to, and I simply said, 'a friend' He snatched the phone and read my texts."

The image of my father, his face hard with disgust, flashes in my mind.

"He didn't even yell. He looked at me with utter disappointment, this coldness. He wouldn't allow my choices under his roof. He said I couldn't risk the family name, and my lifestyle wouldn't bring honor to the family. He told me I had a choice: stay there, stop seeing men, go to North Shore, or leave before graduation and never look back."

My chicken and broccoli sits forgotten. The 'family name.' As if we were a brand instead of people. I can see Dad standing there, calculating James's worth like a depreciating asset. He didn't lose a son that day; he discarded a product that didn't meet specifications. Dad doesn't care about the rules; he cares about his image and control. He forced James out for being gay and me out for speaking the truth. I feel a sudden, sharp urge to reach across the table and take James's hand.

"I told him I would stay. I gave him what he wanted. He hardly spoke to me those two months. He tried to save face in front of you and Mom, but I could tell he didn't even want to look at me."

"But I didn't stop watching him. The way he looked at me, the ultimatum, it made me distrust him completely. I knew he had to be hiding something bigger to justify his own anger."

"Dad kept tabs on more whereabouts those two months, making sure I was at school and work. He didn't know I was doing some of my own digging." James leans closer. "Most days, when you and Mom were cooking dinner, I would sneak into their bedroom, looking for any kind of clue. I noticed

Dad's condom supply diminishing, as well as his pills. I looked them up."

"Ceftriaxone," I interrupt.

James gives me a quizzical look. "That's the one."

"I was fairly certain Dad was cheating on Mom. Everything was adding up, but I had to prove it."

He explains how he feigned sickness twice to get Mom to pick him up early. The first time, no one was home. "A few weeks later, I tried again and bingo. Mom and I came home to find Dad and Kiera."

I recoil. The image of them together still disgusts me.

"All hell broke loose,"

"Dad started yelling at me, telling me I needed to move out right then. Mom kicked Kiera out and told her she needed to leave. Afterward, I started packing up whatever I could in my car."

Piece by piece, details are coming together. It was the day I came home excited for our last family dinner at Gran's.

"I had lost all respect for Dad. He took away my right to tell Mom about being gay. I was still figuring it out. Sharing my sexuality should have been my choice. I didn't know how Mom felt about it because I left as quickly as I could."

He pauses. "But a few months later, she reached out. She said she and Dad talked, and I should visit at Christmas. It seems it was one of her caveats as they started coming to terms with the affair and the aftermath—she wanted me to come each year for the holidays."

A sense of pride in Mom swells up in me. Maybe she is more cunning than I give her credit for. She wasn't allowed to divorce Dad because I was still a minor, so she had to go along with whatever he decided. It explains the depression pills.

"Even after everything came out, why are you living a lie to everyone else? What's the point of you and Brooklyn being together?"

"Look Alex, the first year I was on my own wasn't easy. Dad had kicked me out. Gran wouldn't help. The first few weeks I lived out of my car. I was afraid people at work would notice how unkempt I was. I couldn't lose my job too." Tears form in my eyes, picturing James living in his car.

"Brooklyn was the one who saved me. She offered a place for me to stay. Her parents believe in the purity of the Twenty-Ninth Amendment—the belief it should protect children, even those who just turned eighteen, from neglectful homes. I was lucky they saw my perspective."

As if she heard her name, Brooklyn makes her way out of the office.

I turn my attention toward her. "So your parents know you two aren't really together?" I look from Brooklyn to James.

"I'm sorry, I didn't mean to interrupt," Brooklyn apologizes.

James gives her an encouraging smile. "No, I think you should stay for this part. You're as much a part of it as I am." A smile passes between them. Brooklyn gets a glass of water and sits down next to James, kissing him on the cheek.

Their relationship is a foreign blueprint. I watch the way they communicate—seamless, respectful—a dynamic I've never witnessed. Looking at James and Brooklyn, I realize the state only measures what happens in the bedroom. They don't have a metric for the way Brooklyn leans toward him, or the way James relaxes when she enters the room. Is that what I'm looking for with Silas? A co-conspirator?

I cover up my awkwardness by shoving food in my mouth and checking my phone. I have a text from Silas: "Sorry I couldn't talk. Everything alright?" It's nice having a friend.

Before I can respond, James looks at me seriously. "Brooklyn and I are together. We aren't pretending. It doesn't look the way we were taught it was supposed to look like. I love Brooklyn more than I have ever loved anyone. She is my best friend. Isn't this what partnership should look like?"

He asks me directly. I don't know what love should look like, only what it shouldn't. This might be the closest I've seen to it.

I look at them—two adults who chose honesty over expectation, two people who defined their own terms for love and built a life that works for them, not the government or Gran. This is it. This is the truth I was denied at home: the freedom to define my own reality, even if it contradicts the 'natural' order.

Brooklyn confirms everything. "We may not have the same sexual attraction other couples do, but there's no one else I'd rather walk through life with. We have an understanding, and we've decided it's okay if other people don't get it. We have been planning for a long time to have you stay with us after graduation. What's important to James, like you, is important to me and vice versa."

Their sentiments are sincere. "Doesn't it bother you? Having to hide the way your relationship actually works?"

"Of course. It's frustrating at times," Brooklyn states matter-of-factly.

"I've come to terms with the situation," James adds. "I have a stable job I enjoy. I have Brooklyn, and she understands. I don't need to be the spokesperson for gay rights. I won't be the reason laws are changed." He says this rationally, like he's gone over it a hundred times.

He speaks like a man who has weighed his soul against his safety and found a balance he can live with. It's a quiet life, a hidden life, but it's theirs. I think of the Twenty-Ninth Amendment and how it demands every part of us. James and Brooklyn are giving the state the husk and keeping the heart for themselves.

"We both have decided we can make more of an impact at a smaller level," Brooklyn looks at me lovingly. "We can love and accept others. We can make the world a better place for the people we know in whatever way we can."

She's right. They are making the world a better place for me. Even if their love looks different, I hope one day I can experience a fraction of what they have.

But as far as one person not being able to change the world, I won't settle and agree with James or Brooklyn on that.

I look down at my phone, the screen still glowing with Silas's text. James and Brooklyn have found a place to catch their breath, but I'm still mid-sprint. They are content with a quiet life in the shadows, but as I start typing back to Silas, I realize I'm not looking for a place to hide. I'm looking for a way to outrun the system entirely.

# Chapter 23

Brooklyn drops me off at school early again. Charging toward Mr. Everett's room, the need to speak feels like a physical weight. Silence is no longer an option; he needs the full picture. If he hears one more story, one more piece of evidence the problems are bigger than Lynn, maybe he'll take the next step.

His door is locked, the room behind the glass a dark, silent void. There's still forty minutes until the bell. I walk the halls, searching for Silas. Last night, we texted for hours. I explained bits and pieces of James's story. Silas's own drama wasn't earth-shattering, just his sister, Renée, blowing up after work, sick of providing for the twins she didn't birth. His twenty-four-year-old brother called her a selfish bitch.

I hope the three-year-old twins didn't overhear. It's crazy how much easier it is to talk to someone when you don't have to look at them. Over the course of a few days, Silas and I have grown so close. I can't believe this is the boy I was always intimidated by.

He isn't in his usual spots. I slump against the wall outside of Mr. Everett's room. Knees to chest, earbuds in, the music starts.

After a few minutes I text Silas: "Are you here yet? Meet me outside Mr. Everett's room." The message is delivered but unread. Usually, I'm content with invisibility, but the time drags.

The hall remains empty, an invitation to let my voice out. Singing aloud feels like a rebellion against years of forced silence. The lyrics are a scream of freedom in a world of muted tones. The act is uninhibited—until the sudden weight of a shoulder slumping down against the wall falls next to mine.

I stop mid-lyric. Horror likely registers in a flash, but Silas is already clapping. "Encore, encore!" His cackle is a sound of pure, unrefined joy. The burn in my cheeks is immediate, but his laugh is contagious.

We are face to face, mouths open, laughing, and for once, I think I can read his eyes—read exactly what he's thinking. Time slows. We are in a still frame, and then, in an instant, we kiss.

His breath tastes like the cold morning air, but his skin is warm where his hands find the curve of my jaw. The hallway, the Twenty-Ninth Amendment, the looming shadow of the municipality—it all blurs into the background. The instinct to flee, a constant pulse since childhood, has finally gone silent. I am exactly where I want to be.

After one interlocking moment, we pull apart. My eyes dart around the hallway. It is still empty. A gasp of relief follows. I've been thinking about this for days without acknowledging it, and it is better than I imagined: natural and savored.

But within moments, the gravity of it hits. Silas has a girlfriend. I hated my dad for being a selfish cheater. Yesterday, I screamed at James for a perceived betrayal. Now I am kissing someone else's boyfriend. I am a hypocrite.

Panic flares on my face, mirrored instantly on Silas's. He quickly recovers and grabs my hands. "Alex, don't worry. It was an accident. We didn't mean to do it. It was the excitement of the moment." He says this calmly, but I see he's also trying to convince himself.

But it wasn't trivial to me. It made me feel seen. It made me feel wanted. The guilt descends. I deserve the bad things that happen because I am like my dad—selfish and impulsive. I am trying to build a life based on truth, yet I am as selfish and impulsive as the man I ran from.

Silas drops my hands. His eyes plead. "Alexandria." The full name burns inside me. "Please. You're my friend, and I care about you, but I made a mistake. I can't hurt Mariah. Please."

"Sure. No problem." The agreement is a lie meant to end the moment. Reaching for the bag, the only goal is distance. "I've got to get a head start on the day. Talk to you later, Silas."

The retreat to the locker room is a blur. His silence stings. It means I am simply his friend, and Mariah is more important. Then the guilt settles in again. I am being selfish. Mariah is one of the closest people I have to a friend, and I've betrayed her. I feel dirty and shameful. I need a shower.

Hot water hits, but the soap can't touch the regret. The kiss plays on a loop: longing, followed by the crushing weight of betrayal.

"Hey Alex," Mariah says, walking in. You have got to be kidding me. I force out a hello. She unloads her gear. "I'm excited for today's meet. I know we've already secured regionals, but today is great practice for this new tactic." She is chirpy, maybe more than usual, but my guilt is probably warping my perception.

"Yeah, it'll be good," is all I can manage. I head for the door.

"If you wait for me, I'll walk with you to first period." Shit. Statistics.

"Um, I forgot I have a meeting with my guidance counselor about college," the lie flies off my lips. I hope she misses the stutter.

"No worries. I'll see you for the meet later," Mariah waves.

Once I make it around the corner, I collapse to the ground. The events of the morning overpower my independence. It was silly to think I could make a difference. I've never had friends. Now I'm tearing people apart without them even knowing. My breath is short, and tears brim. Facing Mariah in first period is an impossibility. The only move left is to disappear.

The run past the Municipal Records Office is fueled by adrenaline and self-loathing. Tucked into the corner of the municipal parking lot, surrounded by chain-link, is the stark, prefabricated unit. A small sign reads: 'Regional Compliance Screening Center.'

Before I know it, I am standing in front of my parents' house. The neighbor's holly hedges provide a vantage point.

Within minutes, Mom emerges in her scrubs. She drives away, a silent ghost.

Dad, Kiera, and the girls walk out about fifteen minutes later. Savannah's hand is in Dad's; Charlotte's in Kiera's. They look like a cohesive unit.

Dad bends down and hugs Savannah, then Charlotte. I can't remember the last time he hugged me. Dad opens his car door, then turns and kisses Kiera.

The instinct to scream is a fire in my throat, but it's quenched by the realization that I've already played the hypocrite today. I take the sight and bank it as fuel.

Once they vanish, the run continues toward Gran's. The massive oak tree provides cover.

Ten minutes pass before a car pulls to the curb. Principal Sterling steps out, adjusting his tie as he walks up the driveway with the familiarity of a frequent guest.

The fear is a sudden, icy jolt. Does he know I skipped class? Is he here about me breaking my promise of obedience? I don't wait to see him reach the door. The run back to campus is a frantic sprint. A stupid kiss has put everything at risk. And I'm the only one to blame.

Every footstep on the pavement sounds like a gavel. I've handed the municipality the perfect weapon to use against me. I was more than impulsive; I was reckless. I traded my safety for a feeling that's already curdling into shame.

The return to school takes eight minutes—a personal best. The lie to the secretary is practiced: "Sorry, I'm late. I was helping with my little sisters this morning. Their mom wasn't feeling well." The use of 'their mom' is a calculated move. She nods, hands over a pass for third period, and the doors close behind me once again.

# Chapter 24

Class is a blur of oscillating thoughts: Principal Sterling at Gran's, Dad kissing Kiera, Silas and I kissing, the meet, the possible alliance forming. The bleachers are the only escape for lunch, the autumn chill acting as a natural barrier that keeps the rest of the student body away. Behind the seal of my earbuds, invisibility isn't just a habit anymore—it's a power.

The rest of the day goes quickly. The closer it gets to the last period, the more impatient I become to talk with Mr. Everett. Then, anxiety hits about seeing Silas.

The History wing feels off. No rhythmic lecture spills into the hall; no smell of Mr. Everett's stale coffee. Inside, a substitute stands where he should be. The sinking in my chest is a physical anchor. Behind the desk, the woman is a blank slate of indifference.

"Excuse me miss, do you need something," the substitute asks while I hover at the door.

"Where's Mr. Everett?" I blurt out, the question thick with panic.

"I'm sorry, I don't have that information." To her, this is just a period to fill; to me, it's a vanishing act.

My heart starts to slow. "Of course. I'm sorry. I was worried; he's never been out before." I make my way to my seat, and then my heart starts to race again. Silas and I make eye contact.

"Hey, Alex. It's weird Mr. Everett's not here, right?" Silas says casually, acting as if nothing happened. I'm thankful for his normalcy, but it stings. It confirms the kiss was a mistake and my feelings are unreturned

"Yeah, really weird. Where do you think he is?"

Silas opens his mouth, but the substitute cuts him off. "Good afternoon class. Congratulations! You have made it to the last period of the day. We will start by reciting the Twenty-Ninth Amendment." My lips move, but my mind is elsewhere. Is Principal Sterling at Gran's related to Mr. Everett's absence?

When the bell rings, Silas turns. "Alex, we should talk."

"I can't right now. We're about to leave for the meet. I'll talk to you later though," I turn my back and rush out.

---

The secretary's desk is a gatekeeper, but a single word—urgent—forces the lock. Principal Sterling emerges from the inner office, a wall of tailored suit and authority that makes the room feel small.

"Hello, Alexandria. The bus for the meet leaves in five minutes. Surely you shouldn't be here."

"Yes, but I wanted to check in beforehand. I noticed Mr. Everett wasn't here today, and we normally meet after school."

"That's very responsible of you. Consider it a day off. Mr. Everett should be back tomorrow."

He says it with a smile; the words feel like a trap. What if Mr. Everett isn't 'off,' but he's missing? I look at the pass in my hand, the ink still wet, and wonder if the school is already erasing him the way my father erased James.

Believing Principal Sterling is the only choice for now. A sprint to the bus follows.

Coach Vance stands by the door with a digital clipboard, frowning at us. "Check your gear, ladies. DPUs charged and clipped on," he barks. He doesn't care about our feelings; he cares about compliance.

The aisle is a gauntlet of gear and teammates. Ashley and Alicia are already paired up. "Alex, there's room here," Mariah says, patting the seat next to her.

An empty diagonal seat further back offers a temporary reprieve. "Thanks, but I'm on a deadline. I've got to finish this data set."

Mariah's smile remains unwavering. "I understand. We can't let up yet."

The music is supposed to be a wall, a way to zone out the world, but the defense is thin. A tap on the shoulder shatters it. My bag is moved to the floor, and the seat beside me is suddenly occupied. Mariah slides in, a Statistics book already open in her hands.

"I figured I could help you with what you missed this morning. Turn to page fifty-seven."

The window is a cold, glass wall on one side; Mariah is a wall of relentless kindness on the other. Every chirpy explanation about inferences and samplings is a direct hit to the gut. "See, this is how the government uses population data and survey sampling to support the Twenty-Ninth Amendment." The math is simple, but the irony is a gag in my throat. I am the data point that doesn't fit the curve.

The bus hisses to a stop outside Everett High School—a merciful end to the lesson. Relief is a sharp intake of air. A huddle forms on the pavement where Coach Vance reiterates the strategy: the lead belongs to Mariah and me. "Look to Alex and Mariah for communication."

Mariah takes charge then, her voice clear and authoritative as she leads the count. "1, 2, 3—"

"Rams!' The unison shout echoes against the side of the bus.

The starter's gun fires. Mariah and I find our stride side by side. Right before the two-mile mark, I increase my speed and Mariah moves alongside me. This is my favorite part of any run. I hit my stride. I'm in the zone, laser-focused.

The final stretch opens up, a narrow lane of gravel and grit. Maximum speed is the only gear left. A quick glance sideways to signal the shift to Mariah reveals nothing but empty air. She's gone. Somewhere in the blur of the last mile, I lost her. Slowing down now would be detrimental.

The finish line passes in a blur, the sprint giving way to a jagged, lung-burning jog. Coach Vance is already moving, his face a shifting map of confusion and rising irritation. 'What happened?' he demands before I can even catch my breath.

"She was there on the last shift," the defense feels weak even as it leaves my throat. "I don't know where she dropped off."

Coach Vance is about to speak when Mariah crosses the finish line. She comes in second, barely, and her eyes are laser-focused on me. She runs straight at me. She veers off slightly, then plants herself in front of Coach Vance, "What's your problem? I'm always so nice to you and then you can't even stick with the plan this one time?"

Mariah is a stranger, her voice raw and unrecognizable. "You have nothing to say for yourself?" The words are a physical sting. I almost wish she had bulldozed me. The amber strobe on her hip snaps into a solid, bleeding red. 'High Risk.' The machine has officially labeled her pain, and I'm the one who provided the data.

I stutter out, "I'm sorry, I didn't mean to Mariah."

"Sorry for what? Sorry you couldn't think about anyone else for a minute of your life? I've stuck up for you so many times and you don't even think about me! This meet could matter for me and the other girls, for our college scholarships. But you don't ever think about anyone but yourself." Tears stream down her face.

She isn't wrong. The one thing I hate about Dad—his self-absorption—is the thing I keep repeating.

Coach Vance finally steps in, "Girls, let's do this later."

"No, Coach Vance, Mariah's right." I look at her stunned face. "I really didn't mean to run ahead. I was all for the plan, but I got lost in my own head."

The truth blurs out before the fallout can even be calculated. It's an impulse—a jagged, reckless heat recognized from a thousand miles away. It's my father's heat. But where he chose the comfort of a shadow, I choose the burn of the light. I love Mariah. I love Silas. And because I love them, I cannot let our friendship become another Eastwick vault. I won't be the daughter who builds a life on a foundation of secrets.

"I didn't mean to hurt anyone. I am so selfish. I didn't mean to hurt you, Mariah. You've been nothing but nice. I'm an awful person. I didn't mean to kiss Silas this morning. I swear it was an accident."

The words fall out. My confession solidifies the guilt in my gut. Mariah's face falls.

"Mariah, please," I whisper.

"Don't!" The shriek is raw, her voice cracking under the weight of the betrayal. On her hip, the DPU's amber pulse snaps into a frantic, rapid-fire strobe. The red light is a rhythmic scream, a digital bleeding wound for everyone to see.

I did this. I turned her into a 'High Risk' data point. I am my father's daughter after all, breaking people and leaving the evidence for the government to find.

Waiting for the inevitable explosion isn't an option. The retreat toward the guest locker room is instinctive, a blur of motion fueled by the need for distance.

The school bus is no longer a possibility—not after the fallout. Everett sits closer to Boston than Lynn, which means the only escape route is a public stop a few blocks away. A sprint through the cold ends just as the bus pulls from the curb, leaving nothing but a cloud of exhaust. Thirty minutes. The wait is a sentence. A slump onto the metal bench sends a shock through the sweat-damp uniform, the cold biting deep and fast.

Fury is a cold, hollow weight. The regret isn't just for the words spoken, but for the audience that heard them. Silas called the kiss a mistake. Maybe it was true for him, but my feelings are real. I couldn't live with the guilt. I don't want to be like my dad. Mariah is nice; she doesn't deserve to be cheated on. Honesty was the right move, but the timing was a disaster.

A vibration rattles against the metal bench. Mariah. The expectation of a barrage—curses, accusations, a digital scream—is almost a relief. Anything would be better than the unknown.

One deep breath later, the screen glows with a single message: "Coach Vance wants to know where you are. We're waiting for you on the bus."

Her message is so nonchalant, so civil. Am I being dramatic? I type quickly: "Tell him you can go without me. I'm going to take the public bus home." Then I quickly add, "Thanks for checking." I figure I owe her decency.

The sun is setting, and the air is cold. I check my phone relentlessly. No response from Mariah. She must have been forced to text me by Coach. I stare at the street. I woke up so excited to see Silas, to start fighting for something bigger than myself. Now I messed that up with a stupid kiss, and I screwed up the meet for everyone.

I still have fifteen minutes until the next bus. Mariah's words from the meet ring true. "You don't ever think about anyone by yourself." It mirrors her first encounter with me in the hallways, but now I have given validity to her claims. I realize how much I am thinking about myself, making myself the victim. She's right.

A sudden buzz against my thigh breaks the loop. The expectation is more Mariah, but the screen displays a name that hasn't appeared since Friday: Mom. The timing is a cruel joke. A mother—the kind who offers a hug or a lie like 'it's okay'—is exactly what the moment demands, but that person hasn't existed in years.

The call goes ignored. It's immediately followed by a second attempt. A sharp thumb-press to the side of the phone kills the vibration, but a third buzz starts before the screen can even go dark. This time, the phone is shoved deep into a coat pocket, out of sight but still thrumming against my hip like a frantic heartbeat.

The bus finally arrives. I'm thankful for the heat. I'm chilled to the bone. The bus is nearly full. I find a seat next to a middle-aged woman absorbed in her phone—a safe spot. I take out my phone to start my music and notice the third missed call wasn't from Mom, but Silas. I also have a text: "Alex, please call me."

Silas's message isn't hateful, but his vagueness is unreadable. He must be pissed that I told Mariah. He told me not to.

Still no response from Mariah. I text her again: "I'm really sorry Mariah. You don't deserve this." Apologizing is the least I can do. In one day, I ruined the one friendship I was forming and the possibility of one with Silas.

The 'delivered' icon stares back at me, a tiny digital indictment. I want her to scream at me, to call me a hypocrite, to be as loud as I was with James. Her silence is worse.

I put on my oldies playlist, but it doesn't alleviate my heavy emotions; it intensifies them. The music creates a sense of nostalgia for Gran's house, for singing with James, for when the family felt whole. Was it ever really like that, or was I ignorant?

My phone buzzes a fourth time. I can't ignore it. It's James.

"Hey James, I'm on my way home. What's up?"

"Mom called me worried about you. Your Coach said you ran off after your competition. Where are you?"

"I'm on the bus. I'm going to take it to the T and then I'll be home." Something James said registers. "Wait, why did Mom know to call you? Did you tell her I'm with you?" My voice rises, and I lower it immediately.

James cuts me off. "Get off your bus at Sullivan Station. Don't get on the T. I'll be waiting for you there."

The last thing I wanted was to inconvenience James. "You really don't have to James. It's another few minutes to your place—"

He interrupts, his tone resolute. "Alex, meet me at the station." Then he hangs up.

I can't wait for the bus ride to end. James is upset—another screw-up to add to the list. I am making it harder for him and Brooklyn to apply for temporary guardianship, forcing him to leave work early. I managed to do all this within four days.

The bus pulls up to Sullivan Station. James waits at the stop. He looks professional in his heather gray pea coat.

"You could have waited for me in your car," I blurt out, the apology warped into an accusation.

He doesn't respond. He turns to walk toward the parking lot. I follow instinctively, the way I did when we were younger. I want to apologize, to ask about his job, to find out how Mom knew I was with him. But after my tone, I choose silence.

James starts the engine and turns the heat on. The quiet is deafening. It's four miles, but in rush hour, it will take fifteen or twenty minutes.

After about a mile, James breaks the silence. "So what happened? Why did you run off from your teammates?"

His question is unexpected. I anticipated a lecture. James is not like Dad; he is collected and calculating, like Gran. He sees the whole perspective. He asks the deeper question of why.

"Before I get into it, I really need to say I'm sorry for getting Mom involved and that you had to leave work early."

"I actually talked to Mom on Saturday afternoon," he says as a matter of fact. "I knew she'd be worried about you, and I didn't think it was fair to have her worrying about your safety." He adds. "I told her Brooklyn and I are completing the paperwork to become your legal guardians."

This is an honest, strategic disclosure of truth, a direct contrast to Dad's life of lies, yet guilt forms in the pit of my stomach. I wonder if this will crush her. "How did Mom take it?"

"Mostly, she seemed relieved that you were safe. But from her frantic phone call today, she must have been pretty shook up on Friday." He circles back. "So why did you run from your team today?"

"It's a long story," I say, still avoiding the conversation.

"Good thing I've got time," he smiles back.

I start with the meet. "We had a plan for our final meet today. I was supposed to sacrifice my PR and run with Mariah. The idea was if I helped her, everyone's PR would improve."

"You didn't mind that?"

"No. We already secured regionals. Anyway, I got lost in my own head while I was running and completely lost Mariah in the last stretch."

"It sucks, but since you've already secured regionals, is it really such a mistake you couldn't ride back with them?"

"Mariah was really upset. She mentioned her college scholarship and then she lost it on me. And I didn't help myself. I was already feeling so ashamed from kissing her boyfriend this morning. When she started verbally attacking me, all of the guilt started to bubble over and I told her I kissed Silas."

"Wait, you kissed her boyfriend?" James says this more confused than accusatory, which makes me laugh. He chuckles along with me. The lightness is welcome.

"It just happened. An accident," but then I remember Silas's words. "Actually, Silas called it a mistake."

"Do you feel like it was a mistake?"

"No, it's the part hurting me the most. I wasn't planning on kissing him. I don't want to be like Dad. But I do care about him and I do have feelings." I've never said this out loud. "Silas has been a really good friend. He listens to me. He affirmed my thoughts about questioning government policies. I think he and I could really make a difference working together; it's the reason I told him about you and Brooklyn."

There's an immediate, seismic shift in the atmosphere. "Alex, you told him you're staying with Brooklyn and me, right? It's all you told him, right?" James unbuckles and turns toward me, the key idling. His body language is completely different. I am frozen.

James is losing his composure. "Alex, what did you tell him about Brooklyn and I?"

"I only told him a little about your relationship —the basics. But he won't say anything. I swear. He has his own family stuff."

"Alex, I want you to live with Brooklyn and me. We have been planning this for a long time. I want you to feel safe. But I thought it was obvious I want the same for myself and Brooklyn. You shared personal business we intended to keep private."

His words hit harder than any lecture from Dad ever did. James isn't punishing me; he's mourning the trust I broke. I look at the floor, the invitation to live with them feeling less like a rescue and more like a second chance I don't deserve.

"You're right. I didn't think about it. I won't do it again, but Silas is trustworthy. He won't say anything."

"Damnit Alex. You're not getting it." He's not yelling, but his voice is stern and disapproving. "Not only did you tell someone else, but you said you were planning to do something bigger with the help of this kid. This implies you were going to share it with whoever was going to help you."

He removes the key from the ignition. I want to tell James about seeing Sterling at Gran's house, but I've lost the right to share secrets. I've turned the truth into a liability.

"You're so busy trying to save the world, you don't care who you burn to do it," he says, slamming the car door behind him.

I am left alone, my ego wounded even more than it was before, the silence of the garage now deafening. I look at my reflection in the darkened car window. James is right. My desire for truth and justice is poisoned by my own reckless self-centeredness. I don't look like a rebel. I look like my father's daughter.

# Chapter 25

My alarm drags me from sleep. All I want is to sink back into the mattress. Maybe if I fall back to sleep, yesterday will dissolve into a dream.

Life has been a steady deterioration since I was eleven, since the day Dad's infidelity and Kiera's pregnancy shattered our world. James moved out without explanation; my assumption was he abandoned me. Mom became emotionally detached; our routine of cooking turned rote and joyless. I didn't know she was depressed. Kiera moved in. The house dynamics shifted. Charlotte and Savannah became the center of attention. No one thought to ask what I needed.

Outside the home, the town gossiped. Dad couldn't hide his affair; he moved Kiera in as if she were a trophy, a sick sign of conquest. I feel physically ill thinking about it. At school, kids mimicked their parents' scorn. I felt even the teachers judged me.

I got used to it. I found ways to cope, to fly under the radar. I made myself invisible, doing just enough in every class, in every interaction, to avoid attention. My one exception was running and look where it got me.

Everything started to go wrong the moment I spoke up in Mr. Everett's class, the moment I thought I deserved more. I wish Gran hadn't stepped in; maybe a government watch list would have been better. Now I am caught in a chain of unchangeable events.

If I had stayed silent, I wouldn't have been pushed to the breaking point by Dad's punishments. I wouldn't have run away, and Charlotte and Savannah would still have me around. James and Brooklyn wouldn't be inconvenienced.

Now my safe place, Gran and Gramps' house, is gone. I long for the smell of Gran's food and the comforting stickiness of the photo album pages, but that safety is stripped away. I know too much now: Gran's complicity in James's forced exit, her secrecy, her use of power to undermine the law. I crave comfort, but naivety is dead.

I used to think the Municipality was the only one capable of erasing a person. Now I realize my own family has been doing it for years. They didn't just hide James; they buried the truth of why he had to leave, and in doing so, they buried me too.

If I were still ignorant, I wouldn't know James's struggles, his sexuality, or the truth about Dad kicking him out. I wouldn't have pissed James off with my selfishness. I wouldn't have anything to tell Silas.

If I had stayed silent, I wouldn't have befriended Silas or trusted Mr. Everett. I wouldn't have let them in. I wouldn't have made the mistake of kissing Silas.

It was all a mistake. I am a mistake. I am utterly hopeless. James and Brooklyn, Silas, Mariah— they all took pity on me, and all I did was hurt them.

I turn off my alarm, curl up under the blankets, and try to will yesterday away.

"Alex, it's time to get up." Brooklyn's voice is muffled from through the door. "We have to leave in fifteen minutes."

I can't imagine how she can even speak to me, let alone sit in a car with me. I didn't stick around last night; I took a shower, went into my room, and skipped dinner. I was too embarrassed to face her. But they communicate about everything. She knows.

I can't afford to be selfish. James was right about that. Poor attendance will look bad for their guardianship application. I have to go.

I throw on sweatpants and a hoodie. I don't bother with a shower; I shove a beanie onto my head.

Bare minimum. I wait five extra minutes, decreasing the risk of running into James. I grab a banana—my stomach is clenching with hunger—but I don't want to spend any more time in the apartment.

Brooklyn and I get into the car. My stomach is in knots, mostly from nerves. She is kind, but she can't read me the way James does.

She puts the music on low, an oldies station. I am thankful for the background noise and the lack of small talk. The objective is simple: survive the day's encounters with Silas, Mariah, and the team. I am awkward in social situations, but this is worse. I know I can't skip school, but I consider skipping cross-country practice. Having me on the team feels like a distraction now.

I wonder if Mr. Everett will be back. He doesn't know about the last two days, but I suspect he doesn't want to know.

"Oh, I love this song," Brooklyn says, turning up the volume. She starts singing along. I recognize it immediately—one Gran plays—but the depressing lyrics and slow, wistful tone are why I never learned the artist.

"When did it end? All the enjoyment. I'm sad again," Brooklyn sings.

I prefer uplifting music distracting me from reality. This song is a downer. I feel tears forming. I fight them back, wishing I could feel nothing. I force myself to stop the pain. My eyes are glassy, but nothing falls.

"Think I forgot how to be happy, something I'm not, but something I can be," Brooklyn attempts the soft tone as the song ends. She smiles.

She turns the volume back down. "It seems sad, but the song is actually hopeful." I stare forward. I can't look at her right now. "Right now life could seem a certain way, but the song holds onto the idea that things can change."

She's forcing the narrative. I'm not sure what's worse: James's stinging honesty or her unbelievable diplomacy.

I say nothing. I can't risk sounding sarcastic. I am trapped in the car, but I can retreat back into my shell, making myself less visible

---

I get to school and head straight for a run. Isolation is safer than conversation; I can't afford any more unstructured time around people. The locker room is empty. Every movement echoes.

I head outside to the course, bundled up against the gray chill. The air is crisp. I can't run the full distance. As I turn back, a light drizzle starts. I hate running in the rain. It feels like the sky is holding in every emotion and then decides to let it out all over me. I am stuck.

The drizzle turns into a steady rain. I run into the locker room, realizing I didn't bring a change of clothes. I strip off my layers. My underwear and sports bra are still dry. I lay my wet clothes on the counter and start using the hand dryer, starting with my socks. The warm air feels nice on my feet, but the rest of me is covered in goosebumps.

As I dry the second pant leg, I hear laughter and giggling. Ashley. I look up and catch a glimpse of them in the mirror: Ashley, Alicia, and Mariah. They are staring at me in my underwear, bra, and socks. Ashley smirks. Alicia stifles a giggle. Mariah's face gives nothing away. I am no longer privy to her feelings.

The hand dryer shuts off. Ashley meets my eyes in the mirror, then turns to the others. "Now all the rumors make sense. I heard she was kicked out of her house. I guess she needs to do her laundry at school now."

I didn't realize anyone knew, but I shouldn't be surprised. Alicia chortles. "Yeah, it's pretty sad when your own messed up family doesn't even want you." They drop the pretense of whispering. They say it boldly. Then they all walk away, leaving me alone, half-naked, cold, and wet.

I finish drying my clothes. I guess this is my life now. No family, no friends. People talking trash right to my face. I deserve it. Brooklyn is the only one still speaking to me.

The day moves slowly. I keep to myself, especially in Statistics. All day, I hear whispers and feel stares. Word moves quickly: my English teacher yells at the class when a girl claims I was doing my laundry in the sink. The teacher gives me a death stare, even though I am silent. Everything feels like my fault.

I stare outside. The rain slams against the windows. The wind moves the branches violently. The thunder and lightning interrupt the teachers with loud rumbling. I should have stayed in bed.

I know avoiding Silas is impossible in History. I pull my hood over my head and keep my eyes on the ground, trying to shrink. Before I enter the room, Mr. Everett steps out and summons me with a finger. He looks different today—not the frantic lecturer who used to gasp for air between sentences about national pride, but a man who spent his day off staring at the edge of a cliff. His movements are slow. His usual crisp shirt is slightly wrinkled at the collar.

"Alexandria, Coach Vance wanted me to let you know practice is canceled today due to the weather."

"Oh, okay. Thanks." One problem is solved.

"We will resume our studies today. Since you don't have practice, we'll start right after the bell rings."

"Sounds good." A single bright spot.

The bell rings. Mr. Everett turns to enter the classroom. I follow him and see my empty seat. Silas's seat next to it is vacant. He's missing. Did he intentionally leave for the last period to avoid me?

Mr. Everett clears his throat, a sharp, clinical sound that cuts through my thoughts. I am standing at the edge of the classroom, staring at the deserted seats. Everyone is watching me notice Silas is gone. So much for being invisible.

At the end of class, I stay behind. "Do you know where Silas is?" I blurt out.

"I don't know of Mr. Wright's whereabouts any more than you do." He hands me a pile of papers.

"We're going to shift from discussion to reading and research. Start making your way through this pile." He doesn't look at me as he says it. He's already turning back to his desk, adjusting a stack of folders with a precision that feels like a lock clicking into place.

So much for being the highlight of my day. I am being willed back to silence. Another adult who prefers not to hear me.

Thursday slams into place, a monotonous gray blur. I am moving through the apartment, my body on autopilot. The tension with James is a tight, silent wire stretched between our rooms. I ate alone last night, avoiding him. This life with them was supposed to be the answer, but it hasn't even been a week, and I already feel the friction of a failed experiment.

Cross-country ends tomorrow. I am still debating whether to show up for Regionals. It was always a long shot, but after Tuesday's incident, a win is impossible. My only certainty is graduation. It is the single escape route, the one way to ensure a future, regardless of the consequences here.

If it takes sitting across from Mariah in Statistics, I will do it. If it means enduring the deafening silence of Mr. Everett's required after-school reading sessions, I will comply. I will do whatever it takes to appease Principal Sterling and receive my diploma. Then I will leave. I will start over somewhere far away, where no one knows the shamed family name and where I can't put James and Brooklyn at risk.

My rides with Brooklyn have become easier. She is still pleasant, but she talks less and plays more music. Perhaps she is picking up on my social patterns, or perhaps she is simply tired of the drama. Whatever the reason, I find comfort in the contained quiet of the morning drive.

She pulls up to the curb. I have forty-five minutes until class. I can't linger outside, and I can't risk the locker room. I know Brooklyn is watching in the rearview mirror, waiting for me to enter before she rejoins traffic. I push through the double doors.

Mr. Everett's room is the only refuge.

He sits at his desk, engrossed in a stack of papers. I knock gently on the door frame. He looks up, his eyes weary.

"Alexandria, what can I do for you?" His tone is not cold, but still distant.

"I'm sorry to bother you, but I was hoping I could sit in the back some mornings and read through those papers you brought." A pause stretches the air. I rush to fill it. "I promise I won't bother you. I can put in my earbuds." I need this connection. It's the one thread of normalcy I have left to hold onto.

"Sure, not a problem." He gestures toward the back.

I sink into the cluster of desks, turn on my music, and grab the top folder. This document is dated 2033, with the letterhead of Senator Wolf's office. It is preliminary research for the Twenty-Ninth Amendment. I scan the pages, my eyes snagging on the enclosing stamp: "From the desk of Elizabeth Davis." Lizzy. My Great-Grandmother. I knew she helped with the Amendment, but I didn't know she was President Wolf's secretary.

My appreciation curdles into a frantic fervor as I read. The document notes the positive impacts–decreased environmental strain, economic growth—but I focus on the "Possible Public Concern" section.

One bullet point details how the Amendment discriminates against the psychiatric, intellectually, or physically disabled. A note, written in sharp handwriting, is scrawled beneath it: 'Goal = decrease' with a check mark.

A check mark for a human life. A tally for a stolen future.

Then I see the bolded title: LGBTQIA+.

The term is unfamiliar. In our textbooks, there are only two categories for relationships: "Productive" and "Non-Compliant." I've spent my life learning that any deviation from the nuclear family is a biological error—a drain on the Republic's resources. But this acronym isn't a clinical label. It looks like a code. A hidden language for a group of people the Twenty-Ninth Amendment didn't just ignore, but actively tried to delete.

I start to look up at Mr. Everett, the question rising in my throat, but I stop myself. Don't bother him.

I plunge into the research under the bold title. It outlines the detrimental impact on people who prefer same-sex relationships. My blood runs cold. Beside a paragraph about the "phasing out" of these communities, my great-grandmother's handwriting reappears: 'Social contagion risk. Mitigate through sterilization benchmarks.'

They knew. The government knew the risks and harm it would cause, yet they pursued it anyway. The irony—my great-grandmother crafting the oppression my brother now hides from—is a burning sickness inside my stomach. They didn't just overlook the harm; they calculated the harm. The Amendment is fundamentally a tool of eugenics and prejudice, built by my own blood.

The family loyalty she preached was a mask for active cruelty. They didn't just comply with the system; they built the flaws into the foundation. And yet, Gran protected Dad, protecting his lineage, even when he defied the law with Kiera.

My hands are shaking. My insides rage. I want to scream at Mr. Everett, shake this damning document in his face. "See this is why we need to do something!"

I close my eyes and take a deep breath. I count to five on the inhale, five on the exhale. Don't react. Impulsivity leads to disorder. I breathe again, forcing the ache in my stomach and the frantic pace of my heart to settle.

The bell rings. I am lost in the pages. I am not ready to face anyone. I act on a desperate impulse, one I can't contain. "Mr. Everett?" I wait until his eyes meet mine. "Do you think I could stay here today and work through these papers?" The question is earnest, eager, betraying my need to hide.

He gives me a quizzical look, sincerely considering it. He puts down his pen and sighs. "I'm sorry Alexandria. As much as I'd love to help you out, we don't want to draw any more attention to ourselves than we already have. You should go about your day like normal."

We? I am not the only one in trouble. "Did Principal Sterling—"

Mr. Everett cuts me off, his voice soft but firm. "Alexandria, I'll see you this afternoon when you're finished at practice."

I nod in understanding and let myself out the door as his first period students begin to file in.

He isn't mad at me; he is scared. The distance I sensed isn't rejection—it is self-preservation. He is choosing his stability over the fight. My thoughts are racing as I make my way to Statistics. I am so distracted I almost run into Mariah in the doorway.

"Sorry." The apology spills out, the ultimate irony.

We are inches apart, the closest we have been since the blow-up. Her lip part, then snap shut. She turns away, walking to her seat.

It could have gone worse. I sit down and mentally prepare myself for the day. I will do exactly what Mr. Everett said: Go about my day as normal. I will not draw attention. I will put my head down, do as I'm asked, and avoid any confrontation.

I distract myself with the documents. I do the work required in class, but my mind is filled with the question of why Wolf ran on a campaign he knew would hurt so many people.

I make it to History. Silas is absent for the second day in a row. Hope and fear clash in my chest. I pull my phone out to text him.

"Alexandria, don't you think you've been in enough trouble as of late?" Mr. Everett gestures toward my hand holding the phone.

I feel like an idiot. "I'm sorry Mr. Everett, it won't happen again," I say dutifully. He walks away without another word.

Texting Silas will have to wait. I spend the rest of class attentive, hoping Mr. Everett will notice my repentance.

When the bell rings, I get up to head for the locker room. Mr. Everett stops me at the door. "I'll see you after practice Alex," he says, his tone a clear reminder of my duty.

"Thank you, Mr. Everett. See you then," I respond, trying to convey my reverence.

The moment I open the locker room door, the chatter stops. Everyone's eyes are on me, then they snap away. They pretend I don't exist. Good. I walk to my locker, putting my head down. I'd rather be invisible again.

I make it out to Coach Vance without incident.

"Let's huddle up, team!" He gets straight to business. "Run your warm-up first." Groans and sighs ripple through the group.

"C'mon, everyone put your hands in. Mariah, lead us."

Hands pile up. I toss mine into the center. It takes what feels like an age for another hand to touch mine. Mariah exudes a distant confidence. She yells, "1, 2, 3" and everyone responds at once, "Rams." We take off to start the warm-up.

"Alexandria, c'mon back." Coach Vance's voice is calm, but I freeze.

I turn around and jog back. "Yes, Coach?" I muster an agreeable tone.

"I'm glad to see you're here today. There's no excuse for your behavior, but the truth is, we need you. The metrics show me what you're capable of. I don't expect us to win tomorrow, but this is an important meet for many of your teammates. I'm hoping you can put aside your own problems for the next two days and act like the leader and teammate I know you can be."

His words are pleas, but I hear the command. This isn't a choice. Just like with Mr. Everett, my Gran or Dad—this is an expectation with consequences.

I've learned my lesson. Impulsivity leads to disorder. I must be calculated. "Of course Coach Vance," and I run to join the others.

# Chapter 26

I wait until the last echo of the team dies in the locker room before I emerge, clean and feeling strangely powerful. I head toward Mr. Everett's room, a knot of confidence and urgency tightening in my chest. I made it through the day without incident.

Silas was absent today, so I can focus on the files. The preliminary research I read this morning ignited a sense of mission. I refuse to stand by, like Mom has done. But I can't be reckless, like Dad. There must be a plan.

Gran's words resurface: "To preserve order, we must keep an accurate account of history."

Mr. Everett's papers are history. I know there is a lever to be found in those documents.

Mr. Everett sits at his desk, his concentration so intense he remains motionless until my backpack thuds softly on the back table. "Oh," he clears his throat, startled. "Hi, Alexandria."

"Hi, Mr. Everett," I smile, a brief, controlled gesture, and get straight to work. He seems to appreciate the silence and returns quickly to his papers.

I find the last page I read. The document on the Twenty-Ninth Amendment ends. The next file is thick and labeled "China's One-Child Policy." I scan the pages, looking for the critical link. Senator Wolf's administration, including my great-grandmother, used this data to argue for population control and economic growth. I note the reasons the One-Child policy was terminated in 2015—low birth rates, gender imbalance—but I see no mention of its impact on minority populations.

I pause, my eyes tracing the steep decline on the demographic charts. My education was a long drill in efficiency. I've spent years analyzing bell curves and population densities for my Benchmarks. The manipulation in these files isn't subtle to someone who was taught to build them. In the 1980s, China's birth rate fell from nearly six to under three in a decade. It was "successful" data. Now, her own government uses those same curves to justify the 29th. It feels like a dead end for my research, but a beginning for my understanding. I rush through it.

Mr. Everett is still absorbed. I grab a file from the bottom of the stack, labeled "School Board Meeting Notes." The letterhead is Lynn Public Schools, dating back nearly sixty years. I check the attendance lists.

None of the names are familiar until I see one: Tyler Sterling. Not Principal Sterling, but surely related. I flip forward, my fingers moving faster. I stare at the memo's footer. It's signed by Tyler Sterling, but printed beneath the signature line, a formal stamp reads: "Eleanor Eastwick, School Board Liaison, Compliance Oversight Committee." Eleanor. It is Gran's name—the name my parents use for legal forms. The one I rarely hear.

The word 'Compliance' jumps off the page, cold and familiar. It is the same word the Municipality uses now to enforce the Twenty-Ninth Amendment. I realize then this board functioned as a strategic testing ground. Gran wasn't just observing; she was helping build the infrastructure of control decades before the first forced surgery.

I flip through the pages, my mind automatically sorting the data into the 'Cost-Benefit' grids we've been practicing since primary school. Like everyone else in my grade, I was taught to see these numbers as the math of a healthy State. But seeing my Great-Grandmother's signature on the same curves we studied in Statistics changes the perspective. It's one thing to calculate a demographic decline on a whiteboard; it's another to see the ink where your own bloodline authorized it.

I trace her name for six years before it vanishes. She was on the school board when Dad was a kid? Was this the origin of her power, the start of her rise to Massachusetts Secretary of Education? Her secret meetings with Principal Sterling at her house can't be a coincidence. After the revelation about her mother, I won't believe this is a fluke.

I clear my throat, "Mr. Everett?"

He looks up, waiting. "Did you know my Gran was on the school board a long time ago? Her name is on some of these meeting notes."

He sets his papers down. "No, but it makes sense. She was Secretary of Education when I first started here. She never mentioned it to you?"

I shrug, embarrassed by my family's history of silence. "What about Tyler Sterling? His name is on the minutes for at least ten years, maybe longer. Is he related to Principal Sterling?"

Mr. Everett stands up and walks over, bending over my shoulder to look. He flips through a few pages, his expression concerned. "This is too small of a district to be a coincidence. There must be a relation."

He starts to walk away, then stops. "This is good, Alexandria. Work your way through those documents, specifically when your grandmother and Sterling were both on the board. See if any agenda items stick out as odd."

"Wait, Mr. Everett, is there something specific I should be looking for?"

He is already back in his chair. I pushed too hard. I see the conflict in his face: the need to reprimand me for the breach of silence versus the urgency of the moment. He takes a deep breath and puts the pen down.

He moves to the back of the room, sitting in Silas's empty chair across from me. His eyes dart to the hallway, then back to me. He doesn't look like a teacher anymore. He looks like a man who has spent the last forty-eight hours weighing his life on a scale. He lowers his voice to a bare whisper. "I wanted to wait for something solid, something useful."

I wait.

He grips the edge of the table, his voice thin but steady. "I've spent my life teaching you about the sacrifices of the past. I'm realizing I'm terrified to make one in the present. But I can't look at these desks anymore and pretend the history I teach is the truth."

He looks at the door, then back to me, as if weighing whether my silence is something he can truly bet his life on. He seems to find the answer in the files spread between us. He lets out a breath and closes the gap between us.

He leans in, muttering. "When I wasn't here the other day, I made a trip to Philadelphia to visit an old friend. She's the one who gave me all these files."

"So you weren't mad at me?" The relief spills out, making the situation immediately about myself. "I thought Silas and I might have gotten you in trouble."

He smiles, and lets out a heart, but suppressed, chuckle. "Of course I wasn't mad at you. And you didn't get me in trouble, though caution is warranted. You and Silas sparked something in me I hadn't felt in a long time." His tone turns serious. "I've been repressing my anger, pushing down the betrayal I felt from the government, from the Twenty-Ninth Amendment, for years. It wasn't until last week the wound was reopened."

He tells me again about his unsuccessful surgery, the nurse who told him the doctor made a mistake, and his desperate follow-up with her years ago. "I knew I wouldn't be able to drop it unless I could talk to her." He recounts waiting outside the hospital until she left work, how she recognized him and wasn't scared.

"We talked for hours. I wasn't the first patient of hers with a failed reversal. It had happened a handful of times in the few years she worked there. She couldn't prove anything, but she felt like it was intentional. She meets underground with others—nurses, people from all fields—to gather evidence against the government. They call themselves 'The Order.' She thought if I shared my experience, they might uncover something new."

"But you moved here over eight years ago. Why wait until now?" I am baffled by his history of inaction.

"I met with her once—Maria. I left overwhelmed. I felt small. I didn't know how I could make a difference, and I didn't want to face the government's wrath." He confesses his surrender, a mirror of James's own weariness. "I locked that part of my life up. She gave me her phone number and I just never used it. Until last week."

"Does this mean what I think it means?"

"It means things have changed a lot in the last ten years. They've made a lot more progress and connections. Maria gave me some documents when I visited her. She also hooked me up with one of her friends here in Greater Boston who is part of the underground revolution. I got most of these papers from him Tuesday night." He leans closer. "They're actually meeting tomorrow night at the old library. I'm planning on going, but I was hoping I'd have something of substance to contribute."

This isn't just a handful of disgruntled people; it's an organized movement. My individual suffering is a piece of a larger, collective fight.

"Isn't it risky to have all of this here?" I ask, glancing at the files containing the research I discovered.

"Probably, but since Principal Sterling has me meeting with you and Silas every day, I figured it could easily be under the guise of research and patriotism."

Hearing Silas's name snaps me back to the present. I grab my phone out of my bag and dial his number. Mr. Everett watches me, puzzled but silent. Silas doesn't answer. I text him: "Everything okay? Haven't seen you. I have a lot to tell you. Call me."

"Sorry. You just reminded me. Silas hasn't been here. I wanted to make sure he's okay."

"I've noticed Mr. Wright's absence, but I haven't heard anything. Selfishly, I was hoping to have you both here. In the paperwork from Maria, there is a list of names of failed surgeries, mine included. I was hoping you and Silas might come across something of interest in your research."

I finally see what I can contribute. My own experience, Silas's questions, Mr. Everett's failed surgery, the documents showing my family's involvement, Gran's possible corruption– it all converges. I can make a difference. The law isn't meant to stay the same. We can't go on the way it is. The Twenty-Ninth Amendment served its purpose, but now it's hurting more than it's helping. Life isn't meant to stay the same. We evolve, and so should our laws.

I start to open my mouth, ready to pour out everything, but I catch myself. He wants substance. Calculated action is the metric I've set for myself, and meeting that benchmark is non-negotiable.

"I'm in." I close the file folder and slide it into my bag. "I'll take this home and work through it some more. I'll be back in the morning."

# Chapter 27

I barely slept last night. I refused to ignore James and Brooklyn after the disastrous start to my stay. I made them dinner, framing it to myself as a peace offering—an unspoken apology. The truth is cooking is a lifeline. My mind was racing a mile a minute since I picked up those files, and losing myself in the rhythm of creation was a way to destress. It was self-serving.

James and I spoke more than we have since the fight, though neither of us mentioned it. Are we healing or sweeping it under the rug, the way mom does? I tried to enjoy the normalcy, but the whole time I was sitting with them, the internal struggle gnawed at me: I was planning their betrayal. If I wasn't part of the equation, would they feel free to share their experience and make a greater difference?

After dinner, I excused myself, claiming homework. Really, I needed those School Board Meeting Notes. I hoped a solid discovery would negate the need to divulge James and Brooklyn's private life.

I pored over minutes from the six years Gran and this Sterling guy were on the board. Most was tedious, but two years into Gran's term, a voting pattern emerged: Gran and Sterling always voted the same on every issue until she left.

Then there was the curriculum shift. It took multiple public comments and votes. James's words echo: So much of what we learn sounds like the Granisms we grew up with. Gran did most of the speaking for the board on that issue.

The only other anomaly was four years in: "Boston Sterilization Center Partnership." The notes vaguely detail how Lynn Public Schools will provide data to the center and vice versa. There are bullet points about field trips and work training, like what James did in high school. The board passed it instantly, without discussion. It stands out because no other outside partnership ever required board approval.

I stayed up until 1:30 a.m., my head throbbing with information. The shock of Wolf's preliminary research, the One-Child Policy, and now this local corruption makes me feel like I will burst. I call Silas again. No response. My worry spikes.

I drag myself out of bed on four hours of sleep. I am sluggish, but adrenaline is pumping. Regionals and "The Order" are today. I can't wait to show Mr. Everett my findings.

"Good morning Alex," James says, chipper. His energy startles me "Are you ready for Regionals?"

His memory surprises me. Dad and Mom never cared. "About as ready as I think I can be," I manage a wry smile. Compliance is my best defense right now. "Oh, I won't be back until later tonight. The team's going to celebrate how far we've made it this season after the meet. If it's okay with you."

"Of course. Good luck with the meet and enjoy your time with your friends."

Friends. I chuckle inwardly. My only friend is my forty-ish-year-old teacher. "I'm ready whenever you are, Brooklyn," I call out, mirroring James's cheerfulness.

The car ride is a blur of simple questions. I am grateful she doesn't ask for details about my fake celebration; I don't have the energy for more lies.

"Thanks for the ride. See you tonight," I say, practically running out of the car.

I find the classroom light on. Mr. Everett is not at his desk. I turn the corner. He is in the back, hunched over the cluster of desks, papers spread out like a fractured puzzle he is trying to solve. He looks tired, disheveled.

I knock. "Hi Mr. Everett."

He waves me over eagerly, "Come in Alex. Maybe you can help me figure this out."

I walk over. Half-sheets of paper are scribbled with years, labeling each pile of documents. They range from forty years ago to May of this year. Below each year is a list of names. The lists are tenfold the size of the one he showed me yesterday. Some are written in longhand, others are typed on Lynn Public Schools letterhead.

"Why are some of these typed and some written in penmanship?" I ask.

"They're completely separate documents," he says, the words rushing out. "The ones written in longhand are from nurses all over the Eastern seaboard—names of failed reversal surgeries." These are clustered over the last fifteen years. "The Lynn Public School documents are addressed to the Boston Sterilization Center. Maria's friend has an insider who has access there. They're lists of names, all males."

He leans forward. "I don't know exactly what the names mean, but I know all of the students from the last eight years. Look here—"

My eyes follow his finger to the most recent typed list. Near the bottom, alphabetically, is one name that smashes the air from my lungs: Silas Wright.

The moment stretches. Dread makes my stomach clench. I scan the names above Silas's: three seniors who graduated last year, two other kids in our class. I look at the previous year. Silas's name is there too.

"Little overlap exists between the two types of lists," Mr. Everett says, his voice tight with discovery. "But I did find a few names on both." He points to sticky notes next to four names that appear on the Lynn lists nine to fourteen years ago, and on the handwritten notes as recent as two years ago.

"Do you know any of them?" I ask.

"This one," he taps the name from nine years prior: Devin Sullivan. "He was a senior in my first year. He reminds me a lot of Mr. Wright."

The combined worry for Silas and the shock of this list mixes with a sudden painful longing for my friend. "How so?" I ask quickly, trying to mask my emotions.

"Devin was extremely bright but combative. He had a lot of unanswered questions and anger. I had to report him to Principal Sterling. I didn't know how to deal with him back then." A shadow of regret crosses his face.

"You are handling it differently now," I say, truly meaning it.

He lowers the brittle, old list, and I follow the movement of his hand. That's when I see it. A single sheet of paper, heavily redacted, stuck to the back of the list he's holding. It's titled 'Target Assessment Measures - Quarterly Review." Below it, the header clearly reads: 'The Boston Sterilization and Wellness Center."

I stare at the acronym: DPU. Dissemination Protection Unit. Not 'oxygen efficiency.' Not 'funding grant.' It's a metric for the Sterilization Center. They aren't trying to control the 'unfit'—they are weaponizing the health and capability of their best athletes to ensure the removal of the biggest threats. I look at Mr. Everett. "They're not only taking away dreams. They're removing the people most likely to fight back."

The weight of the memo settled over the other documents like dust. High capability coupled with low compliance. It wasn't just data; it was a psychological profile designed to eliminate their future opposition. They needed people to be strong enough to survive the surgery, yet too compliant to question the system.

Devin and Silas weren't just names; they were the proof of the conspiracy's meticulous, cold calculus.

"If Devin is like Silas, it seems like they have a type. If they're sending it to the Sterilization Center, maybe it's a warning of sorts." I look at the clock. Twenty-five minutes have already gone by. We need a plan. "You need to try and get in touch with Devin before tonight," I urge him.

"Alright. I'll try to get in touch with Devin and you get a hold of Mr. Wright. Let him know the plan. We'll meet here after regionals. The Order isn't until 8:30 at the old library."

"Perfect. We'll have time to coordinate before the meeting." Adrenaline and purpose blot out my earlier self-doubt. I'm not just running a race; I'm outrunning a system.

# Chapter 28

I don't know if Silas is at school. I messaged him right after leaving Mr. Everett's room, but the text remains unread. I specified Mr. Everett and I have crucial information and I will see him after the regional meet. I hate feeling like a pathetic stalker, but the message is delivered. Lunchtime is nearing—if he is here, he might see it.

I check the screen again, the blue bubble mocking me. Every minute he doesn't respond is a minute the list in Mr. Everett's office feels more like a prophecy. I'm not just waiting for a text back; I'm waiting for proof he still exists.

Since Regionals are at Marblehead High, we leave ninety minutes early. I'll miss History, but I can't leave until I've accounted for Silas. The only possibility left is the cafeteria.

The cafeteria is both a beautiful and terrible place: floor-to-ceiling windows, hydroponic gardens, and a chaotic hub of clubs and social groups. It is also a battleground of social order. For someone like me, who belongs nowhere, it is a place to avoid. But today, I am on a mission.

I wait a few minutes after lunch begins to enter. I hope the existing noise and commotion will swallow me whole, letting me remain invisible.

The space bustles. My eyes seek out the windows, spotting a long, high-top cafe table where students are studying more than socializing. Reaching it requires a full cross-section of the room. I can't help but observe my classmates: they laugh, joke, and manage to multitask eating and talking with an ease utterly foreign to me.

I stake out a seat with my back to the windows, giving me a view of the room without attracting attention. I'm tracking the crowd, waiting for Silas to come into focus.

Right before I reach the table, I spot him. He is safe. He is here. Relief floods me, immediately followed by a sharp pang of hurt over his ignored calls.

He's sitting there, breathing and solid, oblivious to the fact his name is typed on a list in Mr. Everett's drawer. I want to run to him, but the silence on my phone screen feels like a physical barrier. He chose to be out of reach.

I sit down, open my sandwich, and pull out a book. I pretend to read, but my mind is counting slowly to twenty. At twenty, I give myself permission to look up, scan the room, and glance at him.

He is sitting with Mariah, Ashley, and Alicia. The girls are a predictable toxic presence, but Silas? How can he stand to be near them? They are engaged in conversation.

I go back to chewing my food, counting silently again. I flip a page every time I reach twenty, allowing myself to quickly scan. Nothing changes.

On the sixth cycle, I see him pull out his phone. He has seen my messages. He is choosing not to respond. I want to scream this is bigger than our fight, bigger than him and Mariah. His silence is a clear answer.

I watch him slide the phone back into his pocket, the screen going dark. He treats my warnings like a desperate plea for attention. To him, this is about a kiss, when it's actually about his survival. I can't force him to listen, but I won't let his ignorance become my anchor.

My thoughts get away from me. I am staring. Even across the loud room, Silas must feel my eyes burning into him. He looks up. Our eyes lock.

Shit. I drop my gaze instantly. I can't look up again. My mission is complete. He is here, he saw the message, and he rejected it. I finish my food, cursing my lack of self-control. I get up and walk out the opposite way, putting as much distance as possible between us.

---

I spend the remaining ten minutes of lunch outside on the bleachers, forcing myself to calm down. I can't be rash. Fly under the radar, blend into the architecture—that's the only way I survive the afternoon.

The next forty-five minutes in Anatomy are a blank. I show up, and right now, it's the best I can do. Today is the ultimate test: be the average, compliant student, face the team at Regionals, lead the course, convince Silas, and gather enough information for tonight so I don't have to betray James and Brooklyn. Each piece is dependent on the others.

Principal Sterling' voice books over the intercom—a rare, enthusiastic interruption. "Let's wish our Lady Rams good luck today as they head out for their regional meet!"

As I walk toward the locker room, the DPU clipped to my waistband feels heavy, a silent spy recording my heartbeat. Every stride I take during Regionals won't just be for a trophy; it will be data fed directly into the Center's assessment of my own threat level.

The locker room is buzzing. No one stops talking when I walk in; I am happily invisible. I change quickly and head outside where Coach Vance is by the bus doors.

"Remember what we talked about Alexandria. You can do this." The encouragement sounds like a demand.

I put my earbuds in and sink into the first seat behind the diver, minimizing my interactions.

When we arrive at Marblehead High, Coach gives us a short pep talk. I see Mariah by herself, stretching her hamstrings. There's no more room for avoidance. It's time to face her.

I walk over and start stretching across from her. "Mind if I stretch with you?"

She glances at me, surprised. "Sure," she says. I'll take the simplicity as an uneasy peace offering.

After a minute, I force myself to speak. "I know nothing I say makes what I did better. You were right when you said you're one of the few people who've actually been nice to me. I am really sorry." I pause, letting the silence settle. I came here without a plan, only the knowledge I need for this meet to go well.

I wait for her to look at me, my heart hammering against my ribs. I've spent the week uncovering government conspiracies and family secrets, but standing here, seeking forgiveness from a girl I betrayed, feels like the most dangerous thing I've done yet. If she turns away now, I'm running this race alone.

"I want to make it up to you. Let's run today like we did last week in Lynn Woods." I propose the strategy I ruined last time. "I know we can make it your best individual time."

She thinks about it, her face reserved. Finally: "Sounds like a plan."

We finish our warm-ups. Mariah leads the chant. When the starter's gun fires, Mariah and I are side by side. I will not lose her. I start at seventy percent velocity, tired from lack of sleep but focused on stamina.

A mile and a quarter in, we have our rhythm. I increase to seventy-five percent velocity. Mariah signals the speed shift to the runners behind us. As we hit the two-mile mark, we increase speed simultaneously. We are in the zone. I love this release. My feet hit the ground, pounding away the heartache of the last few days. Even with Mariah next to me, I feel free.

The sensation ends at my waistband. The DPU on my hip chafes against my skin, a constant reminder of my tether. It isn't just measuring my pace; it's auditing my potential for rebellion. Every heartbeat I sync with Mariah is a data point I'm handing to the enemy.

We close in on the finish line. I glance at Mariah. With a nod, we accelerate to maximum speed. I stay glued to her side. The race feels meaningless and essential all at once. We cross the finish line. I see Coach Vance's proud smile in the distance.

I slow to a jog, but Mariah veers off. Her arms fly open, embracing Silas. A genuine, bright smile crosses his face.

I stop. I feel a wave of relief and lightness. He is here. He is okay. Mariah set a personal best. Our kiss didn't ruin them. They are still together.

I put my hands on my knees, breathing deeply. The rest of the team finishes. They offer high-fives and quiet "good jobs" as they pass. It is nice to be seen. Tears well behind my eyes. I feel the victory.

Holliston High won, but we placed third. Mariah set a record. We walk away with a medal.

Before we board the bus, I see Silas and Mariah talking. I yearn to walk over, not out of jealousy, but because everything is going so well. Uncontrolled emotion... Gran would call it a weakness. She says true strength is discipline. Her actions make sense now; she wants to cull the weakness from the system.

I watch them, my fingers gripping the strap of my bag. To Gran, Silas is a data point on a list and Mariah is a peer to be managed. They are what is keeping me grounded. If loving them is a weakness, I'm finally ready to be weak.

Yet the old habits of the ghost die hard. I use every ounce of self-control to turn away and climb the stairs of the bus. I have done all I can. He saw my message; he will make up his mind without my interference.

# Chapter 29

Back at school, I head to the locker room. I don't see Coach Vance, but I see a sticky note tacked to the whiteboard: 'DPUs—Upload Data Before 21:00. No Exceptions. District Policy.' Vance is the middleman, worried about getting his paperwork right. The real danger is at the other end of the upload.

A quick shower serves as a reset before I head to Mr. Everett's room. Composure is a requirement tonight—both to satisfy The Order's scrutiny and to maintain the illusion of normalcy for James and Brooklyn.

I send them a quick text: "We placed third today! Best team time all season. I'm going to be out late, but I'll text when I head home."

Before I even make it to the shower, Brooklyn texts back: "Woohoo! Congrats Alex. Enjoy your celebration." Even her texts exude positivity and unconditional support.

A second text chimes in. It's Gran.

"A strong finish, Alexandria. Your splits show exemplary discipline."

I catch my reflection in the damp mirror. Gran always said I had my mother's eyes, but she added I possessed the strength to control them, not the weakness to let them wander. She never just gave me shelter; she claimed me. The safe space wasn't a home —a perfectly controlled environment where she constantly highlighted my parents' emotional chaos so I would never need to look outside her walls again. Her love was a beautiful, gilded cage.

I stand before my locker, the steam from the shower still clinging to my skin. My uniform is on, but the DPU lies in the palm of my hand—a cold, heavy weight of gray plastic. This device is the tether. It is the silent auditor of my pulse, my pace, and my potential for rebellion.

My thumb hovers over the clip. If I leave it here, the system will flag me within the hour. The 'Ghost' will finally vanish from the server, and Gran will know I've stepped out of the light. But if I put it back on, I am bringing a spy into the library. I am hand-delivering the location of the resistance to the very people who want to erase them.

My heartbeat quickens, a spike of adrenaline the unit would surely categorize as 'High Risk.' I stare at the blinking green light, mocking me with its steady rhythm. I am caught between two deaths: the exposure of my friends or the capture of my soul.

I slide the clip onto my waistband. Not out of loyalty, but as a disguise. I will feed the machine exactly what it wants to see—a steady, compliant heart—while I carry the fire to burn it down.

The realization hits me, solid and clear: I won't betray James and Brooklyn. I won't share their private life without their consent. They took me in. They deserve to tell their own story, when they are ready. I can make a difference without hurting the people who have helped me the most.

---

I arrive at Mr. Everett's room. Silas is already there, talking with Mr. Everett at the back. They both look up as I enter.

All my hard work to maintain composure instantly shatters. "I didn't think you'd come," I blurt out.

"I'm sorry Alex. It's been a rough couple of days." He sighs. "Long story short, after a lot of arguing, my parents agreed to let Renée apply to nursing schools. The decision required a ton of prep and financial planning I had to help with. I stayed home to watch the twins while my mom went to interviews."

My worries about the kiss feel pathetic and small. Silas's world is so much bigger than our mistake.

"Alright kids," Mr. Everett cuts in, his voice awkward. "I hate to break this up, but we have a lot to discuss before we get there tonight. Alex, I was getting Mr. Wright caught up."

"Did you tell him about his name?"

"Being on the list? More than once?" Silas forces a laugh. "I'm not surprised. Whatever this list is, I haven't done too great of a job at going unnoticed."

His self-deprecating humor falls flat against the chilling reality.

Mr. Everett steps in. "I was able to get in touch with Devin Sullivan. Turns out he's already in touch with The Order. He'll be there tonight"

"He shows up on both the school board list and a handwritten list from one of the nurses of the failed surgeries," I explain to Silas.

"We talked for some time," Mr. Everett continues. "He attempted the reversal process last year here in Boston. It didn't go well." Mr. Everett's voice is thick with personal hurt. "Devin was suspicious. He connected with The Order. He has his own theories. He believes schools—at least Lynn Public Schools—are working with Sterilization Centers to provide names of male students they deem unfit for parenthood. For those who meet the official benchmarks, they ensure the surgery is a failure."

"Your school in Philadelphia would have also had to have a similar partnership, right?" Silas asks, his curiosity overriding his fear.

"I'm sure. Politicians everywhere are working together to enforce these backhanded ways to determine who is good enough to be a parent," Mr. Everett says.

"But isn't control the whole point of the Twenty-Ninth Amendment and the benchmarks?" My voice is laced with disgust. Gran is the reason for Devin's broken dreams and Silas's name on the list. Gran isn't a bad person; she's a zealot of purity. But her zealotry is for the Eastwick name first, then the country. She genuinely thinks she's protecting our family's purity by eliminating those she deems 'low compliance' like Silas, while protecting our own 'sins' like Dad's affair. Her purity means limiting freedom for everyone else, and I can't be part of it any longer.

"Why do they think they have the right to decide who's good enough?" I ask, my frustration boiling over.

Silas looks at me, the weight of my words settling between us. For the first time in days, he doesn't look at me as the girl who kissed him. He looks at me as an ally.

"Because people are bigots, Alex," Silas snarls. His anger finally hits, directed not at me, but at the injustice. "If someone doesn't meet their idea of the quintessential citizen, they want to extinguish their lineage."

I think of James. His sexuality is fluid, but his name isn't on the list. I'm thankful, but it just goes to show how human perception is fallible. The benchmarks exist to remove bias from the equation

James survived because he's a better actor than Silas. The benchmarks didn't 'save' him; they failed to catch him. It makes me wonder how many other people are living a lie to stay off a spreadsheet.

"People want control," Mr. Everett says calmly. "They will find a reason to dislike someone. When people in power have too much freedom, they abuse it." He is the living proof: deemed unworthy despite meeting every written benchmark.

I have spent too much time feeling like the victim. Now I'm surrounded by them. "So what do we do?"

"This is why we're meeting with The Order. Devin and the others had theories, but not enough proof. We need to lay out everything we've gathered. It may connect with what they have."

"We need to do something now!" My urgency is frantic. "They're going to keep making their lists and hurting people. The longer we wait, the more people are victimized."

Silas's look mirrors my rage. Mr. Everett sighs. "Alex, I appreciate your intensity, but you're impulsive. And as we've learned, it's not your greatest asset."

The honesty stings. I deflate immediately. I have been working so hard to retain control all day.

Mr. Everett recognizes the shift. He tries to reengage me. "Alex, do you know what your name means?"

"Gran told me I was named after the great American city in Virginia. A sign of patriotism and pride in our country, but also sacrifice and resilience." Embarrassment and shame burn my cheeks.

"It might be true, but your name is deeper than that. It means 'defender of the people.' And Alexandria, Egypt, is known for intellectual breakthroughs. It's a symbol of human potential." His eyes are bright. "We all have our flaws, but we have strengths. You are athletic, independent, and you have a strong moral compass. When we walk in there tonight, let those qualities shine and you will certainly be an asset to The Order."

I repeat the words in my head: Defender of the People. For seventeen years, I was an Eastwick—a polished stone in Gran's collection. But Mr. Everett sees a weapon. He sees a person capable of standing between the people I love and the machine trying to erase them.

For the second time today, tears are forming. I force myself to communicate."Thank you, Mr. Everett."

"So what does my name mean?" Silas butts in.

"I have no idea, Mr. Wright." The tension breaks with shared laughter. We have a plan, we have information, and most importantly, we have each other.

---

We decide to walk the two miles to the abandoned library, each of us carrying a backpack with secrets and files.

As we walk, I don't trail five paces behind them like I used to. I walk shoulder-to-shoulder with Silas. He shares more about his family, his excitement for Renée. He avoids any mention of Mariah, our kiss, or the list with his name on it. I talk about running away and living with James and Brooklyn, avoiding anything too personal. Mr. Everett listens.

"So you want to know what my name actually means?" Silas asks light-heartedly as we near the library.

"I thought you didn't know and asked for a reason," Mr. Everett smiles wryly.

"It means 'forest' or 'wood.' It means I have roots." Silas meets Mr. Everett's eyes, his tone turning serious.

"And why is the meaning important?" Mr. Everett presses.

"It's not," Silas chuckles, the tension instantly dissolving. Mr. Everett joins him, holding the heavy library door open.

I scan the room. About twenty-five people are gathered. The air smells of old paper and cold winter air, humming with the low static of encrypted tablets.

Everyone turns to see us.  In the past, I would have dropped my gaze, wishing the floor would swallow me. Instead, I keep my chin up. I let them see me. I want them to know an Eastwick is standing in their midst, and she isn't there to report them—she's there to join them.

My mind registers the faces: tired, determined, dangerous. These are The Order. This is where the fight begins.

Then I spot her.

The air leaves my lungs. The woman Gran dismissed as a weak liability, stands among them. She isn't the broken mess I was taught to pity or avoid. She is part of the machine meant to break Gran's world. The woman I thought I was leaving behind is already where I'm trying to go.

"Mom?" The word is a whisper, then a breathless exhale. "What are you doing here?"

# Acknowledgements

There is a famous adage: "Write what you know." At first glance, Alexandria's world felt far-fetched and distant from my own. It wasn't until I completed the first draft that I realized how much of my own life was mirrored in hers. Writing poetry has always been a vulnerable, healing process for me, and I didn't expect to find that same catharsis in a futuristic, dystopian novel. Yet, *The Order* demanded the same of me. It just goes to show that even in a world of redactions, the stories we try to hide are often the ones that most need to be told.

**To my students:** Long before I realized it, *The Order* was born in my English classroom. Having taught middle and high school ELA for many years, I've seen firsthand the vital importance of diverse, engaging literature. Reading is the foundation for so many life skills, but if a young reader isn't hooked, that love for stories can easily slip away. I have been fortunate to work in schools that granted me the creative freedom to supplement my curriculum. In 2020, while navigating the laborious task of teaching the Bill of Rights to high schoolers, I did everything I could to make the text come alive—from vocabulary lessons on "unalienable" rights to provocative journal prompts. One day, I asked my students: *If you could add an amendment to the Constitution, what would it be?* I shared my own answer—a mix of humor and a dark sliver of truth. That was the seed for the Twenty-Ninth Amendment. Thank you for laughing with me, questioning with me, and being the inspiration for this journey.

**To my teachers and professors:** Thank you for nurturing my creativity. I know my voice was loud—perhaps at times annoying—but thank you for never quieting it when I wanted to speak up or speak out. Thank you for pushing the boundaries of my writing, for the honest critiques when my conclusions were weak, and for providing a safe haven in your classrooms when I didn't always feel it elsewhere. You taught me that a voice is a powerful thing to carry; I hope I've used mine well here.

**To the YA authors who came before me:** Even as an adult, some of my favorite stories remain Young Adult fiction. From reading classics like *The Giver* and *Brave New World* as a student, to teaching *The Hunger Games*, *Divergent*, and *Fahrenheit 451*, your worlds shaped mine. To authors like Laurie Halse Anderson, Angie Thomas, A.S. King, Yusuf Salaam, and Julie Lee —thank you for your courage. I can only hope this book offers a fraction of the impact your work has had on me and my students.

**To my family, friends, and community:** There are too many to name, but I am profoundly fortunate to have been a part of so many different communities across the many places I have lived. Though the settings have changed, one thing has remained constant: the presence of beautiful people who love unconditionally and lead with honesty. You are the ones who want a better world and are actively creating it through your actions every day. To those who encouraged me to read and write as a child, to those who read this manuscript and saw its potential, and to those who have pushed me to pursue my dreams—thank you for walking this path with me.

**To Charlie:** You still claim you haven't read as many books as you "should." Perhaps if your teachers had been given more freedom to choose literature they were passionate about, things would have been different. But we can start being better now. Change starts with one person willing to push the limits— thank you for being mine.

# Book Club Questions

1.  The Human Lie Detector: Alex says her body is a "snitch" because of the DPU. If a device could track your heart rate and tell everyone when you were nervous, angry, or lying, how would that change how you act at school or with your friends?

2.  The Price of Excellence: In Lynn, only athletes have to wear the DPU. Do you think it's fair for the government to track "elite" people more closely than everyone else? Why or why not?

3.  Gratitude vs. Freedom: The 29th Amendment promises "stability, order, and progress." At what point does safety become a cage? Does Alex's world feel safe to you, or just controlled?

4.  The Biological License: In Alex's world, having a child isn't a choice; it's a reward for meeting benchmarks in age, finance, and career. How does this turn a family into a "business transaction" with the state?

5.  The Vasectomy Variable: The law requires a surgical reversal only after benchmarks are met. How does this physical control over the body change the way people date or choose partners in Lynn? Does it make "love" secondary to

"compliance"?

6. Financial Gatekeeping: One of the benchmarks is financial stability. Does this mean the 29th Amendment is designed to keep the "flats" (the poor) from growing their families? How does this create a permanent class system?

7. The Invisible Barrier: Same-sex marriage is legal under The Order, but because the 29th Amendment controls who can procreate, there is no "surplus" of children. How is this "accidental" shortage actually a calculated move by the government? Is a right really a right if the state makes it impossible to exercise?

8. The Weaponization of Scarcity: By ensuring there are no children available for adoption, the government creates a world where only "traditional" biological pairings can fulfill the human desire to be a parent. How does this pressure people like James to stay "quiet, invisible, and obedient" just to keep the scraps of rights they have left?

9. "Better" for Whom?: The Order claims these laws make a "better world" by ensuring every child has a stable, wealthy, and healthy home. But what is the cost of this "perfection"? If you have to erase people like James or those with fertility issues to achieve "stability," is the resulting world actually better, or

just more uniform?

10. The Definition of "Norm": Who gets to decide what the "norm" is? In *The Order*, the benchmarks are set by people like the Eastwicks. How does this allow the government to "breed out" dissent or diversity under the guise of "public health"?

11. The 29th Amendment as a Weapon: We usually think of laws as protecting people. In what ways is the 29th Amendment being used as a weapon to "redact" entire groups of people without ever having to use a prison?

12. The "We the People" Irony: Looking at the book cover with the Constitution scroll—how do these reproductive benchmarks directly attack the idea of "Life, Liberty, and the Pursuit of Happiness"?

# About the Author

*Dana* grew up in Pottstown, Pennsylvania, and has carried her love of stories and learning across classrooms and communities ever since. She earned her undergraduate degree in English at Arcadia University and went on to complete her master's at Sierra Nevada University. Over the years, she has served as both teacher and administrator in Pennsylvania, North Carolina and Nevada.

Bubbly, sweet, and kind—but with just enough edge to keep things interesting—Dana is a fan of the outdoors, fitness, and above all, not taking herself too seriously. She enjoys hiking, spending time with her husband, dog, and friends, and finding joy in the little adventures of everyday life.

Dana is the published author of *Walk in Dissonance: A Poetry Collection,* a beautifully wrought exploration of cognitive, emotional, and ethical dissonance. Her work blends lyrical sensitivity with unflinching honesty, inviting readers to sit with emotional contradiction and complexity. With her signature mix of clarity and edge, she brings the same sharp voice to her fiction.

*The Order* is her first full-length dystopian YA novel, a bold and thought-provoking story set to resonate with a new generation of readers.

www.ingramcontent.com/pod-product-compliance
Lightning Source LLC
Chambersburg PA
CBHW031025260626
47153CB00017B/2116